Every Time a Bell Rings

Every Time a Bell Rings

Barbara Ankrum

Every Time a Bell Rings

Tule Publishing First Printing, November 2019

The Tule Publishing, Inc.

First Publication by Tule Publishing 2019

Cover design by Croco Designs

ISBN: 978-1-951190-92-7

Dedication

To Jane Porter, for helping me find
my wings and my dreams again.
For being fierce and never giving up.
I can't thank you enough.

Prologue

"I'LL TAKE PARK Place, please. With three hotels."

The pretty young woman with long dark hair sitting opposite Marguerite on the flower-covered bank steepled her fingers together impatiently and pinned Marguerite with a look that said, *Checkmate.*

"Oh, now baby girl," Marguerite mused aloud, shuffling through the real estate cards for the one requested. "Why'd you have to go and do that? I was just about to finally beat you." A sibilant breeze rushed across the lush, rolling meadow of flowers, tilting the flower heads toward them as if each one were listening to their words. The small scruffy dog sitting patiently beside her put his head on his paws with a yawn.

The young woman plucked the required fee from her stack of Monopoly money and handed them to the banker—Marguerite. "I'll make you a deal. I'll sell you Park Place with all the hotels for a dollar. I'll even let you win."

Marguerite flicked a confused expression her way. *Eh?*

"*If* you talk to Roland for me."

Sigh. "Now, you know that's not gonna happen. Anyways, darlin', he won't let you go. It never works that way."

The young woman tossed the card down with a frustrated snap and lined up her red hotels along the Park Place slot with irritation. "Why not? I'm ready. You said so yourself. I mean, look at me. Look at her! She's floundering."

Together they peered down at the faraway woman and young boy rushing to board a plane in a crowded airport. As they watched, all in the space of a few moments, the pretty blonde-haired woman lost track of their boarding passes, spilled her water bottle all over the woman in front of her, and started to cry. Enoch wagged his tail and whined.

"You see?" she said. "Floundering."

Not to mention the young boy, Marguerite thought. He was the true focus of her companion's concern. Before the woman's tears had started, he'd been glued to a screen. For hours. But when his mother began to cry, he tried to comfort her with an awkward, seven-year-old's hug.

It wasn't as if Marguerite didn't agree with her friend's assessment. But her participation was impossible. Rules were rules, and Roland was nothing if not an enforcer of said rules.

"Even if we could interfere, you know why it can't be you," Marguerite chided softly. "Mercy me. Loved ones are not allowed to intervene directly. You're too close, *cher*. And even if you weren't, what we have down there is no junior-league problem. It's a fourth, maybe even fifth-degree problem. Matters of the heart are not easy fixes. They require a deeper change than a simple intervention. And they need a finesse that most beginners simply don't possess."

The young woman paced on the lushly colored bank, sweeping a hand at the mist closing in and blocking her view of the loved ones below. The dog shadowed her with concern, following on her heels. "I should be there with him. I shouldn't even be here. You know the whole thing was a mistake. For both of us. It wasn't our time. Even Roland admitted—"

"No changing things now, baby. No changing things now." Marguerite understood her frustration. She'd been there herself. But that was so long, long ago.

"Look at her. Her choices are so . . . so *human*. Fallible. It will be all wrong for him. If only she'd listened to me, none of this would be happening. She's so stubborn and driven and—"

"And she loves the boy. And you picked her."

"She does. And I did," she admitted gratefully. Sinking down into the riot of flowers at her feet, she plucked one and stripped off the petals one by one. Even as she did, a new petal would replace the last. Tossing it aside, she said, "But she needs help. Even you can see that. She's facing a difficult choice and honestly, I'm not sure which way she'll go."

"Whichever way she goes, she'll watch out for the boy." Marguerite rolled the dice and tossed them across the board. She moved her piece four spaces to Baltic Avenue. "Oh, now you see? I did *not* need Baltic Avenue."

"You're a second order, aren't you? You're only one order away from completion. You could do it."

"No. Roland would *never* let me—"

"Why didn't I think of this before? Of course, it could be you!"

"No, it couldn't." She shelled out a hundred dollars of her money to the bank. "Three houses for my Indiana Avenue, thank you very much." She plucked the houses from the game box.

"Yes, it could," she insisted.

"It won't be me. Your turn."

The look she fixed Marguerite with was a look with which she was becoming familiar. Mercy, this girl was tough.

"Ordinarily," the young woman began, "I wouldn't mention this, but—"

"Mention what?" Marguerite asked, already feeling defensive. Enoch's ears perked up.

"Well, just the other day," she said, delicately, "I overheard Roland mentioning your . . . well, your shedding problem to a Principality. And you know there's only one fix for that. He'd have to agree to let you go."

Marguerite pulled a wounded look and folded her arms beneath her ample bosom. "I do not have a shedding problem." But even as she flounced away from the Monopoly board to stand on the precipice overlooking the scene below, a few feathers drifted past them, spinning in an annoying spiral between them. She quickly batted them away. "All right, fine. Maybe I do. But that's hardly my fault."

"I'm the last one to point fingers, being only a first order. I hardly have anything yet to shed. But I've heard there is a solution."

"An' I suppose you're going to tell me what it is?"

"Confidence. That's it. According to Roland, a lack of confidence is the root of the problem."

"An' just who says I lack confidence?"

A few more feathers drifted between them. Enoch snapped at them.

Propping her chin on the tips of her fingers, the other woman went conspicuously silent.

"Okay, so maybe," Marguerite admitted, "I let that little failure a while back hold me down. That particular situation was a hard loss. But you know, humans can choose and we can only do what we can do. Anyway, a little time off never hurt anybody . . ."

Her companion tossed her a doubtful look.

"Fine. Fine. He may have a point. But even if that's so, this job—" she indicated the woman and boy scrambling to find storage in their overhead bin "—is above my pay grade, *cher*."

"Don't be scared, Marguerite."

"*Moi? Mais non!*"

"Besides, it's Christmas," she pointed out. "When better to intervene than when the world expects miracles?"

She plucked a loose feather off Marguerite's shoulder and

examined it closely.

"All right. All right. I'll talk to Rolan—"

Before she could finish the sentence, the young woman beside her had engulfed her in a hug. "Thank you, thank you, Marguerite! Park Place is all yours. And all the hotels. Forever!"

"Now, now, *cher*, don't get all up on your tippy toes yet," she told her friend, patting her on the back as she might that boy of hers down there. "I only said I'd try. If he'll let me. They must do the hard work. And make the choices. As far as the game? My goal is to win fair and square."

Then with a wink, she added, "But . . . maybe just one hotel. And Boardwalk."

Chapter One

JUGGLING HER PHONE against her ear in the elevator down to the Four Winds Resort lobby, Eden Kendall pulled her seven-year-old son's bright green *Minecraft* scarf from her bag and wrapped it around his neck. Quinn squirmed at her unwanted fussing, consumed with the screen of his tablet and the game he'd been playing since they'd arrived in the High Sierras. And much too often, as a rule, before that. Alone in the elevator with her son, Eden jammed her finger repeatedly against the lobby button. As if that would make the thing go faster.

"No, we're running behind. We just got here," Eden said into the phone, already feeling out of breath. "The airport was a nightmare. Traffic was crazy coming up the mountain. I guess everyone is heading to the snow for Christmas. What little snow there is." She whispered to her son to put on his mittens. If he heard her, he tried to pretend he didn't. "And we're already late for Quinn's first ski lesson."

Nicole Jessup, her best friend and cohort at Wildwood Acquisitions, personal assistant to Wildwood's president and CEO, John Russell, answered, "So . . . I'll tell Monica to tell

Wesley you're right on schedule?"

"You can also tell Monica to tell Wesley to tell his father that next time he wants to send me somewhere on a 'vacation'—" she frowned up at the fresh spruce garland and the mistletoe hanging from above the elevator door "—I could do with a little less Christmas and a little more ocean view."

"Okay, Ms. Scrooge. Some of us actually *like* Christmas."

"What? I like Christmas," she argued. "Well enough." It wasn't that she had anything against the holiday, particularly. It was just that she didn't support the commercialized retail scheme that went along with it.

"I've heard that song before." Nicole sighed. "Anyway, I believe the pipeline to Wesley Russell belongs exclusively to you."

"Rumors and innuendo," Eden said, jamming the "L" button again. Could they make these elevators any slower? Add that to her notes on "resort deficiencies."

"So . . ." Nicole said. "Did you give him your answer yet?"

She glanced down at her son, still glued to his screen. "No."

No doubt Wesley had expected an immediate—if not sooner—swoon and acceptance. But he'd caught her off guard at dinner the other night. She'd never dreamed he'd propose. It wasn't whether she'd say no. It was the *how* she couldn't decide. How to let him down gently when her relationship with him was so intimately tied to their work?

How to not throw the baby—namely her career—out with the proverbial bathwater? How he'd imagined she'd say yes when she'd been carefully backing away for weeks?

If things had been just between the two of them, maybe it would have sorted out differently. But there was Quinn. She'd waited months to introduce them, and when she had, Quinn had made it clear that he wasn't Wesley's biggest fan. That was, perhaps, an understatement. He'd become downright hostile to Wesley.

Because it had been just her and Quinn from the start, she knew a little opposition was to be expected toward any man she brought into their relationship. And to be fair, Quinn had every right to be fearful of change. He'd already been through so much.

And while Wesley knew—had always known—that she and Quinn were a package deal, it was clear to her now that fatherhood wasn't something for which he had any instinct. His interactions with Quinn were awkward, and Quinn felt likewise uninspired to spend time with him. Wesley's attempts to win him over were limited to attending Quinn's soccer games on a Saturday morning with her and spending the entire after-game breakfast trying to talk business with her.

"You know what they say about fools rushing in where angels fear to tread . . ." Nicole warned. "Just sayin'. You're wise to give it some space. But, FYI, he's already leaked word of the proposal."

She felt the blood leave her face. "He what?"

"At least I overheard Monica talking to Peggy, Mark, and Toby this morning in the break room like it's a done deal. Like you're about to send out your 'save the dates.' The rumor and innuendo train will only take on a life of its own from there."

"Oh, no."

"It's only an 'oh, no' if you're going to turn him down. Apparently, he doesn't think that's gonna happen."

Oh, no. "Nicole—"

"You are, aren't you?" she asked, trying not to sound hopeful. "Going to turn him down? Last I heard, you were trying to come up with a way to let him down gently."

She glanced down at her son again. "Right. Honestly. I can't talk about it right now." If anyone knew why she tried to protect Quinn from all of this, it was Nicole. She'd known Nicole for years, since before Quinn and all the changes he'd made to her life.

"Okay." Though Nicole had never said it outright, Eden knew she didn't really approve of Wesley for her. But she never went there. Now, Eden almost wished she would.

"Listen," her friend advised, "just focus on having fun for these few days. Try not to think about the consequences."

The consequences. No, it wouldn't do to obsess about what would happen if she turned Wesley down in what would now be a public embarrassment. She couldn't help but wonder if this was just his way of subtly pressuring her to accept.

The elevator doors swooshed open to reveal the lobby with its vaulted ceiling and spectacular view out the huge plate-glass windows. Decorations were everywhere, from the garland-wrapped banisters to the myriad of trees decorating the cocktail lounge at the center of the lobby. The Christmas elevator music was only slightly improved by the sound of someone playing the same songs on a grand piano in the lobby.

"Speaking of which," Nicole said, switching gears, "how's the resort look? I've heard it's pretty magical there at Christmas."

Taking in the scene, she felt considerably more bah-humbug-y than she had a minute ago. Christmas was everywhere, along with families—mothers, fathers, and posses of kids—all drinking in the cheery holiday atmosphere to the tune of "I Caught Mommy Kissing Santa Claus."

"The only really magical thing about this place," Eden told Nicole, "is how much artificial snow the snow makers are producing on the ski runs."

Quinn dragged himself from his screen to send a puzzled frown up at her. "It's not real snow?"

Eden put him off with a *we'll talk later* look and lowered her voice as they moved through the lobby toward the exit. "I just think Christmas—especially Christmas here—is over-commercialized. I mean, there must be a dozen decorated trees in the lobby and I even saw the ski instructors on the hill here wearing Santa costumes!"

"Aw . . . that's hot," Nicole said.

Secretly, she had to agree. "Yeah? Well, if they're making a list and checking it twice, that list better not end up under the door of my hotel room with suggestions from the hotel gift shop."

"Uh-huh. So, uh . . . Tiny Tim will be right up with your Christmas turkey."

Eden snorted a laugh. "Fine. But one good sign. The crowds here are thin. Just as we'd heard. There should be a lot more people at this time of year. Bad sign for them, good for us."

Nicole went conspicuously silent.

"Nic?"

"I'm here. Well, I hope that all works out for you. I hear they're planning to make you project manager on the redo if all this goes through."

Yes, please. "From your lips to Russell's ears. Anyway, I seriously owe him for letting me bring Quinn along on this business trip. We really needed some time to spend together. Right, Quinn?"

She turned and realized he wasn't there. He wasn't following her. Panic sliced through her. He was nowhere to be seen. Not in the lobby. Not anywhere.

"Quinn?" she called, tentatively at first. Nothing. "*Quinn*?"

"Eden? Is everything okay?" she heard Nicole asking on her forgotten phone. "Eden?"

"I've gotta go!" She hung up, looking frantically around for him, trying not to panic.

The grand, circular lobby gave way to a cocktail lounge located at the center of the soaring room and up a few steps. Huge river rock fireplaces burning fragrant piñon wood formed the lounge's hub, surrounded by sprawling leather couches and low-slung coffee tables cut from giant tree trunks slabs. And everything was decorated for Christmas, from green wreaths hung from the fireplaces to trees colorfully decorated to the hilt all around the room, making it even harder to spot a single, seven-year-old boy. Even at mid-day, the seating area was half-full with guests imbibing or simply taking a break from skiing.

Eden scoured it all, half running, half spinning in circles, looking for him. Finally—

"Mom, look!"

She jerked a look behind her to find Quinn sitting on the floor behind a coffee table and a family of four, petting a brown, curly-haired dog who was bathing his face in kisses.

"Look what I found. Isn't he the best dog ever?" Quinn asked, giggling and ducking away from the dog's damp affection.

Eden took a gulp of air and forced her heart to quiet, but panic had left a metallic taste at the back of her mouth. "Quinn. I-I couldn't *find* you. You scared me. Don't disappear on me like that."

"Oh, I'm sorry," said the pretty redheaded mom in chic après skiwear holding the other end of the dog's leash. "He just wanted to pet our dog. He's fine though."

Now. Now he was fine. But she wasn't. Surely any other mom who lost sight of her child, would feel this panic, wouldn't she? Maybe. And maybe her sweaty palms hinted that she'd never get past overreacting where Quinn was concerned.

Try to relax. This is his vacation, too.

She knelt beside him and the identical twin boys his age whose dog Quinn was petting. The Four Winds was a dog-friendly resort and many dog owners took full advantage of this. There were at least three other dogs here in the cocktail lounge alone.

The place had changed so much since the last time she was here. Upgraded, luxurious. But the smell from the crackling fire brought back memories she'd pushed away for a long time. Memories of a time she'd just as soon forget. Especially now, with everything in her life about to shuffle like a deck of cards.

"I think it's true love," the woman said with a smile, extending her hand to Eden. "I'm Amy. These are my boys, Adam and Zack."

With a nod, Eden took her hand. "Eden. And this, in case he hasn't introduced himself, is Quinn. And he's never met a dog he doesn't love."

"I don't know what we'd do without ours," Amy said. "He's just part of the family. Hence . . . here on the family vacation."

Eden explained, "We just don't have time for a—"

"He's a Goldendoodle," Quinn informed her. "That's golden retriever mixed up with a Poodle." He scrubbed his fingers in the dog's curly fur, his iPad forgotten at his side.

He's seven. How does he even know those dog breeds? She tried to think of a dog—any dog—her son didn't think was adorable. Though she had to admit, this one was pretty cute.

"They never even shed or anything," Quinn pressed.

She gave the pup a scratch between the ears, which garnered her a tender but enthusiastic lick on the hand. Trying for non-committal, she answered, "He's super cute. What's his name?"

"Alexander the Great. Alex for short," Amy answered. "Named for his penchant for conquering hearts."

"And . . . still doing his part, I see." Eden brushed her son's hair back from his eyes. "Thank you for letting him pet Alex, but Quinn, we have to go. Your lesson is starting in a minute and—"

"I don't want to ski," her son complained. "I want a dog."

"Quinn . . ."

"Look at all the dogs here, Mom. People brought them with them. They can stay in their rooms, even. They're no trouble."

Until you had to feed them, walk them, and clean up after them. And if she didn't know better, she'd guess Quinn had slipped that Goldendoodle a dog biscuit bribe to stare at her that way with his adorable golden eyes and his mouth cocked into a doggie smile.

Desperate to change the subject, she said, "Hey, how about after your lesson, we come back and have some hot chocolate? And you can pet all the dogs you want."

"These two," Amy said, indicating her boys, "are doing ski lessons all week. Maybe we'll see you on the hill, Quinn?"

"Yeah!" one of the boys piped up.

"That sounds fun, right?" Eden prompted.

"Okay." He retrieved his iPad and waved goodbye to the twins, then reluctantly dragged himself away from Alexander the Great, who cast a heart-melting look after him. She knew how much he wanted a dog, but for heaven's sake, they hardly had a moment to spare as it was, with work and school. When would they have time for a dog? It was . . . well, impractical.

"Nice to meet you," she told Amy as they got up to go. "Maybe we'll see you tomorrow?"

"Hope so."

TWENTY MINUTES LATER, Eden was sitting at a table in front of the big picture windows that overlooked the bunny slope, watching Quinn weave down the hill. She knew she should be working but couldn't resist watching him try skiing for the first time. His instructor—a hottie dressed in a red ski outfit, complete with Santa beard and hat—seemed to have the patience of a saint, encouraging all four of the kids in his group while adjusting their skis with gentle hands. With her chin on her hand, she watched as he high-fived her formerly recalcitrant son, who seemed to open up more and more as the hour went on and actually seemed to be having fun.

This was a sharp contrast to the boy he'd been lately. Even his teacher had commented on the change. He'd been distracted. Stressed. Unhappy. She'd tried talking with him but couldn't seem to make him open up. He was old enough now to start sorting things out for himself about what had happened so long ago. But he didn't want to talk to her about it. Maybe he was afraid he would hurt her feelings. Or maybe he was mad about everything. Maybe it was none of those things, or all of them.

But on the ski hill, he was transformed.

She found herself watching the instructor. He was tall. That much she could tell behind the Santa getup. And built. And he moved with such grace—skiing backward down the hill, stopping on a dime in front of the children to instruct them. Never for a moment losing control of the four little ones with him. She found herself smiling as she watched him. He seemed to have them all enthusiastically wrapped around his little finger.

And if this sale went through, she was about to put him out of a job.

She straightened with a frown. She couldn't think about that. That was never useful. This was business. Pure business. And it was her job to make sure this place was worth her boss's time and investment.

Still, as she took a sip from her second decaf mocha latte, she found herself staring at the man helping her son, trying to guess what he looked like beneath that Santa disguise. *Ski bros. They all look the same, don't they? Sexy, lean and . . . dangerously attractive.*

In fact, if she just considered him from the neck down, he almost reminded her of—

She sat up straighter. *No.*

Impossible. Not Cole.

He couldn't still be here. It had been eight years, after all, since she'd seen him up here. Not at the Four Winds, but at another larger resort across the mountain. By now, he'd probably transferred his devotion to skiing to the Alps or the Rockies or competing in some crazy ski race somewhere. That's what he wanted, or so he'd said. That kind of life. Not what she'd wanted at all. No, she'd chosen a path that made sense. A normal path with fewer risks. Certainly, fewer wild dreams.

Cole had been a dreamer of big dreams. Too big for her. All she'd wanted was whatever her freewheeling, dreamer parents had never managed to secure for themselves—a stable, safe life. And she had it. She'd achieved it.

Nearly.

The job. The man—a certified catch—who checked all the boxes she'd claimed needed checking.

She frowned. *Nearly* all her boxes, that is, except one or two of the more abstract ones, like . . . being madly in love with him, or, even more importantly, him being crazy about her son.

What *did* Wesley really know about her? What she needed, what she wanted, how her list had shifted? They'd never talked about those things. And she had to admit, aside from work and the obvious things they had in common, what did she know about what he wanted?

Did he even want children? His own or, more importantly, hers? They'd talked around that question, but never directly. To be fair, they both deserved that conversation—and a lot of conversations they hadn't had yet—before they even thought about marriage.

At work, they complemented each other. Things she brought to the table, like how her pragmatic, journalistic approach to researching properties complemented his business acumen for recognizing opportunities and structuring deals. If there had been nepotism involved in Wesley's quick rise in the company—and there absolutely had been—no one could argue he hadn't lived up to the task. Since he'd come to work for his father two years ago—after working in finance on Wall Street for most of a decade, the company's revenue and acquisition rate had more than doubled.

Much of that was Wesley's doing. They took failing resorts, rehabilitated, rebranded, and revived them. Or they took them apart and developed the property for other, more lucrative uses. This part of the business had become more and more disenchanting to her. But it was all part of what she did. The fact that her own job security depended on others losing theirs was an irony she could no longer ignore.

For a girl who'd made a career out of knowing exactly where she was going and why, Eden found herself in a directional crisis for which she had only herself to blame. Which was how she found herself, sitting there, staring at some random ski instructor, dressed in a Santa suit, remembering Cole.

She rubbed her forehead. After all these years, she still thought of him. Most often in her dreams. But sometimes, like this, he would pop into her thoughts, messing with her brain. Probably because she'd never fully reconciled her feelings for him. Probably because she knew she'd kind of broken his heart when she'd walked away.

She could still picture his smile. The way he'd made her laugh. Even the way his lips had felt on hers when he'd kissed her.

"Not everybody has that skill, do they?"

Eden jumped at the question that came from beside her and she turned to find a woman sitting there who hadn't been there moments ago. She hadn't even heard her sit down. Good grief. Had she spoken the part about Cole's kisses aloud? "Excuse me?"

"That skill," the woman explained with a wide smile, indicating Quinn's instructor. Her words held the Cajun lilt of some bayou deep in the Louisiana swamps. "Teachin' kids," the woman went on. "Takes the patience of Job. Oh, he's good all right."

"Ah." Feeling silly, Eden nodded, her gaze flicking down the woman beside her. Had she been sitting there for long? How had she missed her? This woman was hard to miss, cloaked in an oversized spruce green wrap, the fringe of which matched her ebony hair and huge dark eyes. In one arm, she held a curly-haired mutt of a dog wearing an emotional support dog vest and in the other, an outrageously tall whipped cream-topped coffee drink. She was smiling at Eden as if somehow, she knew something Eden did not. She had one of those faces that made her age impossible to guess. She could be fifty or seventy. Or anywhere in between.

"I'm sorry, have we met?" Eden asked.

"Not officially, *cher*." She stuck out her hand. "I am Marguerite. Marguerite Ciel."

"Eden Kendall. Nice to meet you." Marguerite's hand was smooth, her skin soft as silk.

"And this," she said, petting her dog's pale fur, "this here is Enoch. Knower of all things, purveyor of *joie de vivre*, and boon companion."

"Hello, Enoch. You're very cute."

Marguerite wrinkled her nose and leaned closer. "He takes a bit of offense at the word 'cute,' *cher*. He considers himself quite worldly."

"My mistake," Eden said, appropriately chastened as Enoch licked whipped cream delicately off his mistress's finger. "I meant handsome."

Enoch wagged his tail at her, and she smiled. She could almost imagine that he understood every word.

"Here for long at the Four Winds?" the older woman asked.

"Not long. Through the holiday maybe. You?"

"Oh. My timetable is mostly fluid. Never know, really."

"Lucky you," Eden said, somehow dreading the thought of returning home to . . . everything. "I have a boss to report to."

"Don't we all?" She gave a conspiratorial wink and took a sip of her drink. A long sigh escaped her. "M-m-mm! Oh, my, my, my! I've missed these so. It just doesn't get any better than a good mocha latte Frappuccino. Am I right?"

Eden glanced down at her cooling decaf mocha latte. "I suppose. Coffee shops. They're everywhere, right?"

"So I hear!" The older woman gave a thoughtful shrug and pointed up at the hill. "A man like that, on the other hand. A dime a dozen he is not."

Eden let her gaze stray back to the man on the hill. She supposed she was right. A good teacher was worth his weight. "This is our first lesson. Do you have someone up there with him?"

"Me?" She laughed, a raucous laugh that made Eden glance at the folks around them, but no one seemed the least bothered. "No, no. I'm just a watcher. An observer, if you will."

"Me too," Eden admitted. "Although that's my son up there. The one in the green scarf."

"Quinn, right?"

Taken aback, Eden stared at her. "H-how did you know that?"

"We heard you callin' for him earlier in the cocktail lounge," she said, as if that should be obvious. "When you lost him?"

Her imagination was getting the better of her. "Oh. Of course." Probably everyone in the whole lounge had heard her. "I was a little panicked there for a second when I couldn't find him." She paused. "Wait . . . *We*?"

Marguerite ruffled the top of the dog's head with a scratch. "Enoch and me. Sometimes he goes off on his own, and I'll just be a puddle of worry 'til I find him. In his younger days, he had a habit of wandering." She leaned closer and whispered, "I'm thinkin' that's how he lost his boy."

A puddle of worry. Hence the emotional support vest, she supposed. Marguerite Ciel was certainly odd, in an interesting way. But maybe she was a little nuts. Eden was sure she was going to regret asking, but . . . "His boy?"

"*Mais oui, cher*. He had a boy once, as all dogs must. Or rather, should. Boys and dogs, you know . . ." she opined. "Go together like shrimp n' grits. But one day, we found ourselves standing on opposite sides of a sliding door. And all I had to do was let him in. That was it. Now we take care o' each other. And he's just fine with that."

If she believed in pet psychics, she might almost believe Marguerite was one of them, the way she went on about Enoch. More likely, she was just lonely and needed to talk. And that seemed the least Eden could do.

But the older woman got to her feet and set Enoch down beside her on the floor. He wore no leash and seemed not to need one as he glanced up to get direction from her. He had on a little silver collar with bells on it, but strangely, they didn't jingle at all when he moved. "Nice to meet you, Eden Kendall," she said. "An' mind, you keep an eye out for sliding doors, *cher*. You never know what'll be on the other side."

Eden watched the pair walk away, momentarily at a loss for words. *Sliding doors?* Strange woman. Harmless, though, she supposed.

Something tickled her nose and she brushed away a downy white feather that drifted away in the draft of the heating vent above her seat. It swirled after Enoch and Marguerite and disappeared.

Unsettled by the whole encounter, Eden gulped down the last of her now cold drink and noticed that the ski lesson had ended, and they had skied to the bottom of the hill.

She hurried outside through the packed snow to the spot where parents were picking up their children from the ski camp. She was thinking about sliding doors as she walked, distracted by the crowded slope full of children and looking for Quinn. She spotted him gliding along beside his instructor, the one in the Santa costume, heading straight for her.

It was the eyes, of course, that gave him away beneath that beard and ridiculous hat. Those kryptonite-green eyes of his with long, dark spikes for lashes that had, once upon a time, made her knees weak, her breath stutter, and her will to walk away nearly falter.

As he pulled off the beard and hat, staring at her like he'd just seen a ghost, he looked just how she felt.

"Eden?"

He said her name as one might if she'd accidentally walked into the wrong room or got caught snagging a bagel from the meeting tray early, or . . . or even the way Wesley had the other night after he'd proposed. *Eden? Did you hear me? Eden?*

"*Cole*?" was all she managed to croak in reply. Dear God. It *was* him. Eight years older. *Eight years better.* His face—always handsome—had an angled beauty to it now with his patrician profile and sun-burnished skin. Tiny lines around his eyes—from squinting in the sun or laughing—only made him look . . . hotter. Where was the fairness in that?

"Mom! Mom! Did you see me?" Quinn was practically

hovering above the packed snow, he looked so excited. "I was skiing! I learned how to snowplow and everything." Frankly, she'd been worried he'd hate it. But no such thing.

Pulling her gaze between them, Eden smiled and opened her arms. Quinn skied in for a hug. Again, an event as rare as a blue moon, lately. "I saw you up there. You were awesomely awesome."

He beamed. "Cole says I did really good. Cole says I could be on the green runs on my next lesson if I want."

She looked back at the man she'd walked away from so long ago. "Is that right?" It was probably just the cold that had her feeling all shivery inside. Or not . . .

"He's a natural. Your son." Cole's gaze dropped deliberately to her left hand. Her bare, left hand, then slid back upward. "I didn't connect the dots 'til now. I guess I'm just surprised to see you here, Eden."

"Ditto." *Oh. God.* Ditto? *You're such an idiot.* "I mean," she corrected, "well, we're here on vacation. A skiing vacation. At least for Quinn. I mean, I'm lounging in the lodge, sipping coffee and reading while he's . . ." He was waiting patiently for her to finish. She swallowed hard. "And you? You're still—"

"—skiing?" He nodded. "I guess some things never change, huh?"

Though he said this with a bit of sarcasm, skiing was technically, *mostly* why they'd broken up eight years ago, she thought. But things had been much more complicated than that. And here he was. Still the same dreamer he was then. His life and ambition still ruled by snow.

Quinn leaned in. "Hey, Mom, do you know him?"

Tugging at the ends of her scarf, she admitted, "We . . . we used to know each other. It was a long time ago." But his handsomeness, that scruff on his chin was distracting her. "Don't you think you should—" she pointed at the white fluff in his hand, "—cover up? I mean, disguise yourself with that beard? For appearances sake?"

In reply, he stuffed the thing in the pocket of his coat. "Quinn here says he doesn't believe in Santa. So, I guess I'm not breaking any fourth wall by taking it off."

Sarcasm again? She couldn't be sure.

"But," he went on, "I told him none of us here on the hill are the real Santa. That old guy doesn't make his rounds until Christmas Eve." To which her son laughed and the two of them shared a complicated fist bump, finger-wag, high-five that they'd clearly choreographed earlier. Some inside joke between them.

She exhaled and an unintentional peep of distress emanated from her throat. "Quinn, honey, why don't you go stack your skis over there, and I'll be right with you. We'll go get some hot chocolate and warm up."

He looked ready to stay all day with his new best friend. But he sighed and said, "Okay. Bye, Cole. See you tomorrow?"

"You bet, Q. You did good."

Quinn puffed up proudly and pushed away with his poles toward the outdoor ski stacking area.

"Um . . . What was that?" she asked Cole, trying to sound off-handed.

Bending down to pop the bindings on his boots, he'd gathered up the skis and took the opportunity to study her face. "What was what?"

"That . . . secret handshake, finger-wave thing you and Quinn did?"

"No secret. Just something I do with the kids to make them feel more comfortable."

"Like calling him Q?"

He shrugged. "Nicknames, joking around . . . it takes their mind off the skiing while they learn how."

"So, nothing to do with trying to convince him that Santa is, in fact, a real thing."

"Not my job," he said, shifting the skis in his arms. "But how old is he? Seven? Said he doesn't believe in the Easter bunny or the tooth fairy, either. A little young to be so skeptical, isn't he?"

"Quinn is . . . he's smart and . . . pragmatic and—"

"Pragmatic. Huh. Big word for a little kid."

And the apple doesn't fall far from the tree was what he must be thinking, Eden mused. She bit her lip to keep from pointing out that all her pragmatism had her here on vacation at a five-star resort in the High Sierras, while he was still teaching at ski school wearing Santa costumes. But that sort of jab fell under the category of unnecessary roughness. "And your point is?"

He looked away, up the hill. "Just that kids his age will believe just about anything you tell them. Even if it's just something that's a little bit magical."

Magical? What good was magic if it simply disappointed you when you found out it was just a trick? No good. That's what. She still remembered getting busted for believing in Santa at eleven, and all her classmates laughing at her. But her parents—with the best of Christmas-y intentions—had steadfastly perpetuated the myth, until her local neighborhood bully, Kevin Mitchell, had not so kindly disabused her of it. "I don't believe in lying to my son."

He nodded, as if conceding the point. "Fair enough. He's definitely on board the *No such thing as Santa* train. We just decided for the sake of the younger kids, that he'd go along with the idea of Santa. You know. Pretend?"

She flattened a look at him. "I do remember *pretend*," she said. "And don't worry. He won't tell the others. He's very kind that way."

"I could see that about him," Cole said. "Must get that from his dad."

She wrinkled her nose at his pointed dig. But quite possibly, that was true.

He shrugged as if none of it mattered one bit. "But hey, you did what you had to. What was right for you. And so did I."

But she'd never quite gotten over feeling wrong about it all. It was only fair that he still held onto a little bitterness about her. Which she absolutely deserved.

But he had been great with Quinn. All she had to do was remember the look on her son's face to realize how long it had been since he'd looked really happy. Never once had Wesley—the man who supposedly wanted to become Quinn's father—elicited that kind of joy in her son. And Cole had managed it all in the matter of what? An hour?

But then, we are talking about Cole Hagan. The guy everyone—including her, once upon a time—loved. Following his heart and the winter season. Determined to be a ski bum for life. Except that he looked happy, too.

As if she'd spoken those thoughts aloud, he grinned at her in that infuriating way he used to when he seemed to mysteriously read her mind. But that was hardly possible. He didn't even know her anymore.

"You look good, Eden. And he's a great kid. You and your husband must be proud of him."

Her uncharitable thoughts skidded to a halt. "I—uh . . . thank you. I am very proud of him."

His gaze raked over her for a long, pregnant moment. "He here with you? Your husband? I'd like to meet the guy who replaced me."

She wound her fluffy pink scarf around her neck a couple more times. "Actually. I'm . . . a single mom."

Cole's eyes widened, but as he opened his mouth to say

something, a beautiful, red-haired ski instructor dressed like Mrs. Claus swooshed to a hard stop beside him, showering them with icy bits before grabbing his arm for balance. Frankly, she didn't look like she needed help with balance, so it was clearly all for show. She did, however, manage a flirty smile for Cole.

"Hey, handsome!"

"Cat."

"Look at you, all decked out. Slumming today?" Cat asked, eyeing Eden curiously.

Did Cat mean slumming with *her*? She resisted narrowing a look at her.

"Santa," he replied, "never slums. Filling in for Kip."

"Lucky little grasshoppers," she murmured, giving Eden the up and down. Awkwardness ensued for a moment or two as Eden considered her escape route. "Oh. Sorry. Hi, I'm Cat," she said, thrusting her hand at Eden. "Didn't mean to barge in."

"No—" Eden began, taking her hand. "We were just—"

"Cat, this is Eden Kendall, an old . . . friend of mine."

Or something like that.

"Eden. Nice to meet you."

"You, too."

"Sorry, Cole," Cat apologized again, leaning against him with a provocative swoop. "But I've been trying to find you to talk about our gig at the concert."

Eden might have imagined the discomfort in his expression as he flicked a look at her.

"Cat, why don't you meet me at Granger's office, and we can—"

Seizing her opportunity, Eden insisted, "No, no, I was just leaving anyway. You two . . . talk or whatever it is you're doing. Thanks for Quinn's lesson, Cole. It was . . . really nice to see you again." And before it got any more awkward, she turned on her Ugg boot heel and headed back to the lodge where Quinn was waiting for her.

But before she'd gone five feet, he called after her, "See ya around, Eden."

Against her better judgment, she turned back and waved. "Y-uh-huh. Sure." But under her breath, she murmured, "Maybe." As she walked, she squeezed her eyes shut for the idiot she was. For the way her heart was racing. For not just saying no. *No, you will not be seeing me around. Or having a drink together. No, you will* not *remind me that Wesley's kisses have never done to me what yours used to and—*

She balled her fists with a groan of frustration.

Ohhh! Too late. She'd already remembered how the delicious slide of his mouth against hers had felt. The scent of the mountains on his skin. The taste of his tongue against hers.

Snow crunched under her feet as she hurried toward the lodge. And she couldn't shake the picture of that irreverent grin of his. The one that held some secret he'd likely never share, clearly best utilized on the lovely Mrs. Claus—good old Cat (Katrina? Catherine? Cat on a Hot Tin Roof?) who was, even as she risked a look back, hanging all over him. His girlfriend? Probably.

See you around?

Not likely. Just what she didn't need was to get distracted by Cole Hagan with that sexiness of his all packed into a hot Santa suit and that mouth of his, making her think about his kisses. The taste of his lips . . . all salty and sweet from a fast run down the hill and . . .

The thought momentarily disoriented her, and she stopped and turned in a half circle, looking for the entrance she'd lost. She found Quinn, waving at her from inside. Pasting a smile on her face, she waved back. No, she would not be seeing Cole Hagan again on this little working vacation of hers. And there would definitely be no kissing.

Definitely. Not a chance.

Chapter Two

EDEN KENDALL . . . back on my mountain again.

Cole made his way toward Granger Stuart's office after hashing out Cat's concerns about the Mrs. Claus getup she was supposed to wear as one of the hosts at the concert. A hot flush of memory about Eden banished the chill from the cold wind stirring the snow up at the bottom of the run.

Crazy, she could still do that to him. Rile up a sweat in him in a matter of minutes . . .

He hadn't seen her in . . . *how* many years? Seven? No, eight. They were both a little older, a lot wiser now. An ocean of water under their respective bridges. Not that the years had been unkind to her. Just the opposite. She looked damn good. Good as he remembered her, only better. He wondered if her hair was still long or if she'd cut it short? Couldn't tell under that baby-doll pink hat she wore. Unbidden, the memory of sifting his fingers through her long, blonde hair came rushing back.

He winced and jammed his skis tails into the snow against the rail outside Granger's office. He supposed it was good Cat had interrupted their conversation. Best to leave that whole situation with Eden alone.

He turned and stared at the door she had disappeared behind.

Yeah. Like hell he would. He wanted answers. Answers she'd never given him.

What were the odds her kid would end up in a group lesson with him, considering how infrequently he filled in for instructors here?

He supposed he was long past being mad at her for leaving. Like all stories left unattended, theirs had mellowed with time. Seeing her again only reminded him of what they'd once had, the good parts. And here she was, with a kid. Still prickly and stubborn. And a mother.

Motherhood looked good on her. But Quinn was seven. And they'd broken up eight years ago. That stopped him in his tracks for a moment. But no, he couldn't be . . . he definitely wasn't his. A little small for his age, Quinn looked half Asian; dark to Eden's light, with a quick, sharp wit and a curious, but encyclopedic knowledge of every bit of Star Wars trivia.

It was more than curiosity about her son that had him wanting to see her again. Maybe just for old times' sake. Maybe there was some end he wanted to wrap up that she'd left dangling. Even though he'd convinced himself he'd tied off all the broken ends of his heart after she was gone. He wondered if she'd managed to follow that rigid roadmap she'd laid out for herself and her future. Had Quinn been a detour or an intentional turn? Did she regret walking away from what they'd had?

Hell.

Why was he even wondering about her? They'd both moved on. Life threw curve balls, but sometimes that's all they were.

He pushed through the outer office door where Sally Haynes, Granger Stuart's longtime assistant, sat at her desk, eating a sandwich as she worked. Mack, Cole's golden retriever, bounded up to him, wagging his tail. Cole scrubbed his fur with both hands and kissed his head. "How's my good boy?"

"He's been waiting for you. Granger's been waiting for you, too." Sally handed him a manila folder of papers as he sat down to undo his ski boots and change into his usual athletic shoes. "And you look fetching in red."

"Thanks. Granger knows I had a lesson, didn't he?"

"You know how he feels about that. That your time is better spent—"

"—running the place from behind a desk rather than from the ski hill."

She tilted a sympathetic look at him.

"Well, Granger's wrong," he said, tugging on his last shoe.

"What exactly am I wrong about?"

Cole wheeled around to find Granger standing in the doorway behind him and he exchanged a look with Sally.

"Old man, you're too damned quiet for your own good."

"All the better to hear my partner complaining about me." Granger smiled good-naturedly and gestured him into his office. Panting, Mack followed automatically on Cole's heels and settled down beside Granger's desk.

Cole shut the door behind him, opening the folder Sally had handed him and scanning the contents. "I wasn't complaining. I was merely pointing out our difference of opinion."

"I like a good difference of opinion. Keeps me on my toes at seventy-two."

"Seventy-two is the new fifty-two."

"If only that were so." Granger sat heavily in the chair behind his desk. "That's why I wanted to talk to you."

"Wait," Cole said, sitting up straighter, a shock of realization jolting through him. "What's this?" He gestured at the folder in his lap.

Granger took a slug of coffee from the mug on his desk. "You can see what it is."

He shot to his feet. "An offer. An offer to buy the resort. What the—?"

"Settle down. It's just an offer. One of four I've received in the past month."

Mack's gaze ping-ponged back and forth between them with something like worry.

"And . . . when were you going to mention them to me?"

Granger leaned back in his worn leather desk chair.

"When I believed it was time to take one of them."

"No." He slapped the folder down on the old man's desk. "No. We are not selling." Times had been hard. Really hard. But they were turning around. Cole knew it. He could feel it.

Granger turned and looked out the window. "Take a look out there, son. What do you see?"

Cole forced his gaze out the window of his partner's third floor office. From here, the view of the Sierras was breathtaking: snow-crowned peaks, granite-faced forests surrounding the Four Wind's ski trails, which bisected the mountain. Each trail was dressed in fresh snow from the snowmakers and dotted with skiers there for the holiday. The snow was late again this year, only bolstering Granger's point. A modest crowd mingled inside the shopping area, its cobblestone walkways and charming shops all decorated for the holiday. There were a few visitors walking dogs. The hotel was dog friendly—one of the changes Cole had made when he'd joined the team. "I see guests. People having fun. Families celebrating the holidays. I see . . . Christmas."

"You know what I see when I look out that window?" Granger asked. "I see Christmases twenty, thirty years ago, with streets and slopes so crowded we had to cap the hill. When our bookings were full two years in advance and there was a waiting list as long as my arm. And every musician and group with a hit record wanted to perform here. When snow fell from the sky and not from the machines we use to suck the lake below dry. I see what it used to be and what it is now. For ten years now, and even before that, our snow was late. If we even got snow. For years now, we've had to make almost all of it."

"Not last year."

"True. Last year was a record snowfall. But it couldn't make up for the years that came before it. And we've lost business to other resorts that haven't signed the Sustainable Trails Charter—"

"—who are still squandering resources and the environment," Cole argued, "which will come back to bite them in the end. Innovation has costs, but those wind turbines we installed on the mountain last summer—"

"—won't pay for themselves for another ten years if we don't get snow again this winter," Granger finished. "Or some miracle. You know that's true. I agreed to the turbines and I did it because you were right to suggest it. We are on the right side of the environment here. With the turbines and the narrower trails and water capture. But, Cole, as a business decision, we must accept facts. We are being buried by the bigger resorts. We aren't recouping fast enough. We're only two-thirds full for this holiday. I'm just saying it's time to consider—"

"No." He said the word more forcefully than he'd intended, but he didn't back down.

Granger leaned back in his chair. "When I took you on as a partner, Cole, it was because I knew my time was coming to an end here. I'm seventy-three next week. It's time for me to retire. I've got enough money saved. I can go without needing to find a soup kitchen."

He would do better than that, and Cole knew it. Granger had done very well for himself over the years here. But he had sacrificed much, too. At his own expense he had protected his employees' pensions and salaries during bad times. Cole knew this time was coming. He just hadn't expected it to come today.

Cole hadn't expected to see Eden today either. And if he wasn't already feeling off balance from that, this pulled out the last stick. He didn't want to talk about his partner retiring. Or about why he and Eden hadn't worked. He didn't want to contemplate the failure of this place when he'd sunk his heart, soul, and savings into it. Buying into this resort was the best thing he'd done with his life to date, and finding a way to make this holiday season successful was his only option now. He had a few tricks up his sleeve with the Christmas concert he was putting on at the hotel's indoor amphitheater. He hoped it would turn the page on the last few years. That much he owed to Granger for the chance he'd taken on partnering with him.

"Don't do anything yet. Give me some more time," he told Granger. "I'll fix this. That's why you hired me. To innovate. Let me innovate us into the future."

Granger tilted a look at him. "After the first of the year, we'll need to make a decision."

"Fair enough. Mack, you stay. I'll be back later." Deflated, Mack sank down beside the desk again and put his head on his paws. As Cole left Granger's office, he was already dialing his phone, and Granger was pulling a treat out for Mack.

QUINN HADN'T STOPPED talking about Cole all evening, through dinner and until she'd tucked him into bed. It was Cole said this and Cole said that until she began to wonder exactly what kind of magic he had used on her son to bring on this bubble of joy. This, in a boy who'd begun to withdraw in the past month or so despite how close they'd always been. Even his teachers had noted the change in him. He'd gone from being a confident, happy kid to the moody child who'd barely spoken to her on the way up to the mountains. They'd even seen a private counselor who had, so far, only told her that Quinn was feeling mad that he didn't have more control over things. *At seven.* But she and the counselor suspected those feelings had everything to do with the fact that his real parents had died when he was three—too young to remember them. This year, he was suddenly old enough to feel that loss. Add that with finally introducing him to Wesley, which that hadn't gone well either, and you had the perfect storm of seven-year-old angst. Both of those subjects she'd carefully breeched with him, but he hadn't wanted to talk.

And yet, somehow, Cole had managed to make him feel like himself again in one short ski lesson.

Maybe it was just that Quinn was away from his usual life. For herself, she had to admit it was a relief to be away from home and all the pressures there, alone with Quinn for some pure fun. Well, mostly fun. Single parenting was hard at best, and sometimes she doubted herself, wondering what her late, great, best friend in the world, Jo, would think of how she was doing as Quinn's mom. Too late now. She and Quinn were going to get through this together. Come what may.

But it was the playing card that Quinn had secreted under his pillow that made her question for the hundredth time what Jo had been thinking to leave Quinn in her care.

"What's that?" she'd asked Quinn. "Under your pillow?"

He pulled a Bicycle-brand queen of diamonds out from under his pillow. "A card."

"I see that. Where'd you get it?"

"He pulled it out from my ski boot."

"Cole did?" she asked, but she already knew. A magic trick? She gave an internal head shake.

"He said magic is everywhere if you just know where to look for it."

"He did, huh?" she said.

Quinn's long lashes shadowed his cheeks. "Don't you believe in magic?" he asked, flicking a searching look up at her.

"Well . . ." She hesitated. "It doesn't really matter what I believe. It's what you believe that counts."

He frowned.

Wrong answer.

Sliding deeper under his covers, he slipped the card back under his pillow. "Night, Mom."

"I love you, Quinn."

Sleepily, he replied, "A bushel and a peck."

"And a kiss on the neck." And she kissed him until he giggled. A few minutes later, from his doorway, she heard him breathing deeply, sound asleep.

She felt the buzz of her phone in her pocket and glanced at the screen.

Wesley.

Her thumb hovered over the answer button, but she didn't press it. She wasn't ready to talk to him right now. She didn't want the pressure of an answer yet and she knew he'd ask.

Instead, she slipped out of her street clothes and into her jammies. Throwing the luxurious bathrobe that the hotel provided around her, she lit the fire and sat in the flickering light in the cozy club chair near the sliding glass door. She stared out at the night-lit ski trails winding up the mountain behind the hotel.

The sky was a star-smattered wash of black velvet hung with a crescent moon. It was a spectacular view, day or night, from this beautiful second-floor suite, with its fireplace and spacious marble bath, so elegant it made her feel rich—which she was not. She could never have afforded a room like this herself. Wesley's father—her boss, John Russell—had naturally made sure his assistant booked it for her. This was business, after all. A write-off, even though he'd kindly allowed her to bring Quinn along. "A good cover," he'd said, and she supposed he was right. No one would suspect her of doing reconnaissance work for her company with her son in tow.

Of course, he'd known about the proposal. She knew that because Wesley had told her he did. John had been a behind-the-scenes cheerleader for their relationship from the start, a fact that both heartened her and made her wary.

For it was a truth universally acknowledged that a woman in possession of a good career should avoid romantic entanglements with men positioned above her. And certainly, with the boss's son.

But somehow, that classic wisdom had eluded her when Wesley had begun to pursue her a year earlier. She'd been flattered by his attention and frankly, a little lonely for adult male companionship. He was a lot of fun when he wasn't laser-focused on work. It had all seemed like a natural progression of their work relationship. He took her out of the everyday-ness of her life which had seemed, before they'd started dating, to be a closed loop of work, Quinn, and sleep.

Rinse, repeat.

Their friendship had deepened, and they had begun to rely on one another at work, sometimes so much that they finished each other's sentences. Outside work, if they went out, it was mostly to dinner or a show after work, but even that happened infrequently. He understood she had a son and maybe she'd used Quinn as an excuse to hold Wesley at arm's length for a long time. It was months before she even mentioned him to Quinn and months more after that when she'd finally introduced them. That hadn't gone well, and it wasn't long before she'd realized she had wandered into dangerous territory with Wesley.

He didn't seem to connect the dots where Quinn was concerned. He tried. But what he seemed to know about seven-year-old boys would fit inside a paper lunch sack. Nor did he seem to realize how much she needed him to bond with Quinn.

And then, out of the blue the other night, he'd asked her to marry him.

Every bit as pragmatic as she was, he'd eschewed words like "love" or "forever" in his proposal. Instead, he'd pitched himself as the man she could always depend on, and her as his perfect match. He wanted to "close the deal" with her and he had the bling to prove it. (A gorgeous two carat stunner that made her throat ache.)

Probably he'd thought the sweet nothings he'd used to propose would sway her pragmatic, practical self. But, in fact, they'd had the opposite effect. And her checklist she'd thought he filled now sat incomplete. Nowhere in that short and to-the-point proposal had he mentioned Quinn. When *she* had, he'd taken her hands in his and said, "Quinn's part of the package. Of course. After all, the kid needs a father, a man in his life. He'll get over his shyness." As if Quinn was an afterthought, when in reality he was Eden's first thought upon waking in the morning and her last at night.

Something about how he'd said it rubbed her wrong. It wasn't shyness. It might have been anger at her for bringing an interloper into their lives. But Quinn wasn't one to voice his feelings. Even at seven, he was like deep, dark water—calm on the surface, mysterious underneath.

She glanced at her sleeping son's room in the dark. It had been just the two of them from the beginning, four years ago. She'd thought it only made sense that he'd be jealous of any man she dated.

But it wasn't until today, until that moment he'd skied down that hill beside Cole, that she'd really understood how unhappy he'd been this last month.

Cole.

She slid down into the chair, curling herself into the memories of him. Eight years and after all this time, she'd never really gotten over him. Not a bit. Oh, her feelings for Cole were different from her feelings for Wesley. He was different than Wesley in so many ways. Where Wesley was all business, Cole was a dreamer. Where Wesley was ruthless, Cole was generous.

And yet, that's the life she'd chosen over Cole. Yes, she would have been broke all the time. They would have lived frugally together in some small apartment somewhere and the life she could have given Quinn would not have been the one she was giving him now. But Cole had told her he loved her. Many times. And his argument against her leaving had nothing to do with practicality or money or success, but only with what he said he felt for her. What he knew she'd felt for him.

She'd never been able to explain her choice to Jo. And looking back, every turn her life had taken since then—apart from Quinn—had been a superficial chase after success. Security. Not her parents' life.

But seeing him today made their history roll over her like an avalanche, knocking her off balance and reminding her that there was more out there. More than Wesley.

There was—

A rap on her door startled her. She hadn't ordered anything. No one knew her here. No one but—

"Eden?" came Cole's voice on the other side of the door. "It's me."

Eden jumped to her feet. It was as if she'd conjured him with her wayward thoughts.

"Cole?" she whispered, opening the door but keeping the security lock engaged.

He was standing there, looking very Cole-ishly handsome, a half-corked bottle of red wine dangling from one hand and a pair of wine glasses in the other.

Out of his red, Santa ski clothes, he wore a pair of sexy, holey jeans and the white linen half-tucked shirt with sleeves rolled up to his elbows. Her gaze fell to his muscular forearms and back up again. She gulped.

"I come in peace," he said, lifting the wine in invitation.

Surprised, she pulled the top of her robe together with one hand. "Wh-what are you doing here? How'd you find me?"

"I know people. I hope you don't mind. I thought we could talk. Maybe have a drink. You can't leave Quinn and I knew I wouldn't run into you down at the bar, so . . ." He shrugged his broad shoulders.

She glanced back at Quinn's room with indecision. Did she want to have a glass of wine with Cole? Talk about things? The past? What good would that do now? He probably hated her.

Wesley's voice echoed in her head. *Eden? Did you hear me? Eden?*

Her answer to Cole's query should be no. An unconditional, definite no.

"Okay," she said, unlocking the door and opening it wide.

He walked into the room, taking in the cozy fire in the fireplace and the dark, starry view outside the large patio doors. "Nice."

"It is," she agreed. "Very nice. It's a beautiful hotel. You must enjoy working here."

He nodded and set the wine down and poured two glasses, handing her one. "It's not a half-bad place to spend your days. I remembered you like red. Hope that's still true."

She smiled and lifted her glass. "Thanks. I thought you would have gone home by now. It's late."

He clutched his heart. "You thought of me?"

"*No*. I mean, yes." She *tsked*. "Don't confuse me."

He chuckled. "Still got the dimples."

She tried and failed to make them disappear and gestured him to the couch. She sat down there herself, focusing her attention on the flickering flames in the rock fireplace. "I guess they're permanent."

He stretched his arms across the back of the couch. "Like broken hearts, I guess."

She took a chug of wine, working up the courage to ask, "Did I really break your heart, Cole?"

"I never said *you*."

Ouch. "Is that why you came up here? Pay back? To watch me squirm?"

"No." He vaulted off the couch to pace next to the fireplace. "Not exactly. More like to get some answers."

"Answers to . . . what? The meaning of life? Why the tide pulls the—"

"Are you happy now?" he interrupted, those green eyes of his turned on her now, stealing the sardonic wind from her sails.

Was he serious? Did he really want to know? She studied her pedicured toes, freshly polished in a dark, blood red. "Of course," she lied. "I'm . . . happy. I have Quinn. He makes me very happy." That part was the truth.

He took a sip of his wine, watching her over the rim. "Motherhood suits you."

Was that a *compliment*? "Thank you." But she'd never felt as unsure of herself in her life until she became Quinn's mother.

"Surprised me," he admitted.

They'd talked about wanting children someday, back when they were together. But she'd always told him that was a long way off for her. Because she needed to build a career. "Same," she said. "Seeing you, I mean."

"I've moved around some, but I've been here for a while."

She swallowed thickly and took a gulp of wine. "What are the odds, right?"

"I'd say they were pretty good we'd run into each other again eventually."

"Why?"

"Because," he said, "I've wondered about you. Questions like that just need to be answered."

"You wondered about *me*? I imagined . . . I don't know. I thought you hated me."

He drank some more wine. "Hate's a strong word. But I was real mad at you for a pretty long time."

"Still mad?" she assumed. She'd been pretty mad at herself for a long time too.

He took a long while to answer as if deciding then and there if he still was. "Ask me again when we get through this bottle of fine, Napa Valley Cab."

"Fair enough."

Eden, did you hear me?

She stood up and walked to the glass door that overlooked the ski lifts down the hill, remembering the first time they'd met at a fraternity party on campus, years ago. He was not a frat boy and she was anything but a sorority girl, but they'd both come with friends and had met somewhere in the middle. They'd shared a bottle of wine that night too. Under the night sky. He was studying environmental science, but he was already a competitive skier with a resume of wins behind him. And she was ambitious—a business major with her hopes set on owning a company of her own. Intrigued by his sense of humor, his intelligence, she found herself drawn to him against her better judgment.

"The wine was a good idea. This week's kind of called for a bottle. Or two."

He raised his glass in agreement and clinked it with hers. Their first unilateral agreement. "I thought I saw your parents here in the marketplace a couple of weeks ago. But it wasn't them. How are they?" he asked.

He'd always loved her parents and the feeling had been mutual. "Oh, you know. Jilly and Tom, they're the same old hippies. A little older. Still hugging trees and lecturing me about you." His eyes flicked to hers, as if he wasn't sure if she was just taunting him or not. She wasn't.

Cole smiled slowly.

She loved her crazy, funny parents to death but she worried for them and always had. She'd known, early on, that if she didn't take care of them when they got old and broke, after not saving for retirement, who would?

"They may be crazy," she told him, "but they're my crazy."

This, he acknowledged with a dip of his head, offering her a breath-stealing view of his Chris Pine-esque profile. There was more angle to his cheekbones now, more shadow on his stubble-covered chin. His mouth curved into a smile that made her think of days spent lying together in the sunny mountains in the summertime, watching the wind move the clouds. Welcoming him as he rolled above her, blocking the sun, and leaned down to kiss her.

He swirled the wine in his glass, lost in thought too. Finally, he said, "Jilly must love being a grandma."

Relieved to be pulled out of her illicit thoughts, she said, "Oh, she's over the moon about him. She's been teaching him macramé and the joys of a good patchouli/sage room cleanse. And they watch Star Wars together. All three of them." She shook her head. "It's a mini-cult."

"I got a little of that from him today, up on the mountain." He joined her at the door. "If I remember correctly, your dad had a genuine light saber from the set of one of the original movies."

She pressed her index finger to her lips. "A proper prop man. He's saved it all these years, hoping he'd have someone to give it to. Now, it's going to Quinn when he turns ten."

He traced an imaginary zipper across his mouth and glanced at her through those dark lashes of his. "My lips are sealed."

Running her finger over the rim of her glass, she said, "I'm sure you've done the math. But don't worry. He's not yours. But then, I guess that's pretty obvious."

That little questioning line between his brows again . . .

"Technically, he's not mine either," she added. "Although he belongs to me now."

"Now that requires an explanation."

She nodded and exhaled deeply. "You remember Jo?"

"Jo . . . your college roommate, Jo?"

Just saying her name recalled the flashes of joy she'd brought to Eden's life. The hundreds of silly times they'd had on campus at UCLA and in Westwood, cocktail waitressing together at Yesterday's just to make tuition. That day she'd stood beside Jo as she'd married Aaron, the love of her life. She and Jo had wound up in distant cities, but never lost that close connection.

"That's the one. She and Aaron—you probably remember him too—"

"Their wedding? You and me? You sat at the head table

with them and I sat with her great aunt Eunice at a table somewhere in East LA" He smiled, remembering. "But we had a good time, Eunice and I. Rehashing the economics of the Great Depression." He lifted his wine to her memory.

She laughed softly. "She was always very fond of you. Then there was you, Aaron, and his second cousin, Thomas, smoking cigars at the cigar bar—"

"Damn good cigars they were too."

"—singing Alpine skiing songs in the middle of July."

"We got a little bit drunk. And you and I danced."

The memory of holding him came back to her so viscerally, for a moment she had to look away.

"To . . . what was that song?"

"'My Wish,'" he said. "If I recall correctly."

The Rascal Flatts tune became "their song." At least for a while. "I can't believe you remember that."

"I have a shockingly good memory. About a lot of things." He straightened, his face suddenly losing color. "Wait. Wait a minute—" He was starting to put the pieces together about her son. She could see it on his face. "Quinn?"

She nodded. "Jo and Aaron had a baby a couple of years after their wedding. A beautiful little boy. And one night, when he was just three, they got a babysitter and went out to special dinner on the beach in Malibu. They never made it home."

He swore. "Oh, no. I'm . . . oh, God."

"From what we could put together, a car—probably a drunk driver—hit them and forced them over the side of Malibu Canyon Road. They both died. And that little boy they left behind was Quinn." She took a long, fortifying sip of wine, her eyes tearing up. "I was his person . . . in the will. There really was no one else. Her parents were gone by then and his still lived in Singapore and were older. Too old to raise a baby. And so, Quinn came to me about four and a half years ago."

"Wow." Cole leaned his head back against the glass. "Wow."

"Yeah. It was a *wow*. I mean, I never imagined when I agreed to be their go-to person—"

"—nobody would."

"—right? But Quinn . . . he's turned out to be the absolute best thing in my life."

He rolled his wine glass between his hands and leaned a shoulder against the doors. "I can see why. Lucky kid to have you."

"That's surprisingly kind of you to say, but the truth is, I question myself all the time." She'd never told anyone that before. Not Wesley. Not even Nicole. Maybe she told Cole because this was just a one-off. After tonight, they'd go their separate ways and tie up that last loose thread between them. And that would be a good thing.

"I imagine every parent questions themselves. That's how they get it right."

"But how do you know if you're getting it right, or royally screwing them up for life?"

"We survived, didn't we?"

She leaned her head back against the glass door. Cold seeped through the glass. "And you? Married?" He wasn't wearing a ring, either and here he was, in her room with wine. Which didn't mean anything. At least she hoped not.

"No wife. No kids," he said simply.

"Your friend Cat looks ready to step into the job."

That pulled his gaze up to her. "She's just a friend."

Hmm. "Does she know that?"

"We've gone out a couple of times. That's all. I'm utterly single. That surprises you?"

"Honestly, yes. When I thought of you . . . *if* I thought of you," she corrected, "it was with a wife, two point five children, and a golden retriever. The family that skis together stays together, or something like that."

"In a teepee on some mountain somewhere?"

She blushed and laughed. "Not exactly."

"Admit it. You did. Or chasing good snow around the world."

"Well . . . that. Yeah." That had, in fact, been their undoing.

"You'll be relieved to know the teepee never came to pass. The snow, for a while—yes. But the dog . . .There is a golden retriever. His name is Mack."

Of course there is. "Quinn loves dogs. He . . . desperately wants one."

He poured more wine and took a drink. "So, get him one."

She shook her head. "Impractical. We hardly have time for homework, much less a dog. Besides, my landlord frowns on pets of any kind, most of all the kind that bark."

"Every boy should have one."

"You know, you're the second person today to tell me that." With a shiver, she imagined long walks during a dark, stormy night on poop patrol.

"Kids need someone to dream with. Quinn seems like he's ripe for that."

This pushed the obvious button with her of raising an only child. She was one herself and was raised with sibling envy. But she said, "You don't really know him. He's very—"

"Pragmatic. So you said."

Self-contained was the word she was searching for. No, her son was not like her. He was her polar opposite. But more and more, she saw that open part of him withdrawing from her. Until the mountain. Until the lesson with the man standing beside her. He had brought out something else in her son. Something he'd misplaced.

"Does he make lists too?" Cole asked, raising his glass.

A little jab. "He hates lists, actually."

"A boy after my own heart." He watched her over the rim of his glass. She watched him back, noting the muscle twitching in his jaw, the curl dangling carelessly across his forehead, and the gold flecks in his green eyes.

She said, "Lists can be useful, even to dreamers like you. I still make them."

His smile became wistful. "And somehow, I fell onto the wrong side of all of yours."

"Not all of them," she blurted before she had the chance to stop herself. With a wince, she looked away.

He reached for the bottle and poured her more. "As I remember it," he went on, "your lists had some pretty tall ambitions attached."

"There's nothing wrong with ambition. It's gotten me to where I am today."

"Which is . . . where exactly?"

Eden turned and stared out into the darkness behind the pane. "Where I should be. Where I always wanted to be." She was, wasn't she?

"Good for you, Eden."

She wasn't quite sure if he meant that or not, but she nodded, not wanting to compound that half-truth with another.

Only a few inches separated them as they stood against the cold glass door. Yet, she could feel the heat of his arm near hers. Smell his skin. Soap and water and . . . that utterly delicious scent of him. She could sense him staring at her even when she looked away. God, she'd made a mess of this. But after all, nothing would come of this simple shared glass of wine. She couldn't let it.

"Regrets?" he asked suddenly, downing the last of the cabernet.

So many. Too many to count. Mostly, she regretted the empty space that separated them now. Regretted wanting to kiss his mouth and taste the wine on his lips. But here she was, on the brink of achieving all those things she'd wanted for so long. And all she could think was she'd missed a step somewhere.

She shook her head. "Um . . . nope."

From his expression she guessed he'd rather she'd chosen door number two in answer to that question. *Because behind door number one, Wayne Brady, is an honest to goodness zonk. But thanks for playing!*

"You?" she asked. "Have regrets?"

His gaze wandered to her long hair for a heartbeat, sending heat cascading through her, before whatever she'd glimpsed in his eyes flickered away. "Right now, it's that this wine is gone, and my dog's going to be very upset with me for leaving him for so long. So." He set his glass down and sent her a weary smile. "I'd better go. Good to see you again, Eden."

She didn't want him to go. She wanted him to stay. But she couldn't ask for that. She wouldn't.

"Cole?"

Halfway to the door, he turned back toward her. "Yeah?"

"Thanks for the wine."

It seemed like he wanted to say something, then changed

his mind. “Night.”

“Night, Cole.”

And just like that, he was gone.

Chapter Three

COLE USED HIS key to swipe the lock on his room that he kept at the hotel for nights like this one, where he'd had too much to drink. This room belonged to him and no one else, if you didn't count Mack, who had claimed his place on the bed as soon as Cole had walked in the door.

"Good boy," he told him as the dog thwapped the cushy down comforter with his tail.

He stood in the shower for a long time, letting the water pour over him—pressing a hand against the wall for balance, because he felt all off-kilter tonight—then he turned the steamy water to ice cold and inhaled sharply. Damn. He'd never get to sleep tonight if he didn't cool himself off after that encounter with Eden.

He'd come this close to kissing her damned lists right out of her tonight, when she'd stood inches away from him, talking about how happy she was. *Liar.* He didn't know why but he'd always been able to tell when she was lying. Even that last day when she'd said she didn't love him anymore. She'd been lying through her teeth that day. Which was what made her leaving all the harder.

The cold water sluiced over his body until he was shivering and back to himself again. He gave the handle of the shower a vicious twist and shut it off.

Nope, she'd told him. No regrets.

Except her eyes betrayed her with their sadness. She hadn't answered everything tonight. Not by a long shot. Though he'd expected as much. For all her talk about lists and success and goals, Eden was too proud to admit to anything but. And he suspected all was not right in Edenville.

Not that it was his problem. Not at all. She'd listed herself into whatever corner she was in, and she could stay there as far as he was concerned.

He toweled off, rubbed the moisture off the mirror, and stared at his image. He tipped his chin sideways, rubbing it with his hand. Eight years older. He wondered how she saw him now. She'd only gotten more beautiful. But his job was giving him crow's feet and dark circles under his eyes.

Flicking off the light switch, he padded—naked—to bed, crawled under the covers and closed his eyes. Mack sidled over to curl his face under Cole's arm, as he'd done since the first night he brought him home. Cole dug his fingers into the dog's fur, glad to have him there. A warm body. A friend.

He thought of the boy. Quinn. And Jo and Aaron. How short life could be. How cruel. But then he remembered the look on the kid's face when he'd pulled that card from his boot. That pure look of magic.

Eight years. The wheel of time creaked by, with love or without it. He'd spent a long time pushing love away. Waiting. For what? Eden? Well, here she was. What was he going to do about it?

He draped a forearm over his eyes, forcing himself to take deep breaths. He'd think about Eden tomorrow. Or not.

But he fell asleep dreaming about her.

THE HOSTESS AT The North Star, the Four Wind's best restaurant for breakfast, lunch, or dinner, plucked a menu from her hostess stand and smiled at Cole. "Right this way, Mr. Hagan. We have your favorite table all ready."

Cole followed Indigo, a beautiful, young woman with a thousand tiny braids in her short, dark hair to the table by the window overlooking the slopes. The breathtaking view was the draw of this restaurant and guests could watch skiers swooshing down the slopes at all hours of the day.

"Our breakfast buffet is open," Indigo told him as she walked, "if you feel like that, or your waiter can get your usual, if you like. It's Carissa today, and she'll be right with you."

"Thanks, Indi. I think I will do the buffet today. Maybe some coffee."

"Sounds good. I'll tell her." The hostess pulled out a

chair that was backed up to a woman seated at the next table over who was typing away on a laptop and had papers spread across the table. His stomach dropped when she looked up at the sound of his voice.

He was beginning to suspect a conspiracy.

Eden automatically lowered the top on her laptop and shuffled her papers together.

"Making lists again?" he commented, sitting down in his chair with his back to her.

"Are there rules against that here?" she asked over her shoulder.

"I'd have to check on that," he said, turning his coffee mug over. Where was Carissa when he needed her?

He heard her typing on her keyboard again. Maybe she was going to ignore him.

But she said, "Are you stalking me now?"

"I was about to ask you the same thing."

"I was here first," she said.

"This happens to be my usual table. They save it for me." He flicked his napkin open, considering putting it in his lap.

She turned around in her seat. He reciprocated.

"You look terrible," she said, looking suddenly concerned.

He cocked his jaw. "Thank you. You, on the other hand, look great."

"Makeup," she muttered, brushing her hair behind her back. "Hung over?"

"*No*." If she was trying to make him feel better, she wasn't very good at it. "I guess I didn't sleep all that well," he admitted.

She nodded and, after a moment, turned back around and went back to her laptop. She typed for another minute or two, then got up to go to the buffet. He did the same.

On opposite sides of the mirrored buffet, they added to their plates. Eggs, fruit, a waffle. Bacon.

He took more than she did. "Where's Quinn this morning?" he asked across the spread.

"Kids camp," she answered. "I think they're sledding. He needed fun, and I needed to work. A little."

He scooped some potatoes onto his plate. His usual breakfast was oatmeal, and he was going to regret this, but he just kept piling food on so he could keep talking to her.

"I thought you were here on vacation."

She darted a look up at him that reminded him of a rabbit he'd seen in the snow the other day, startled by his sudden proximity.

"I'm . . . yes. I-I'm on vacation. But a little work never hurt anyone."

The phone in his pocket buzzed. He ignored it.

"Just catching up on emails," she clarified, then hurried back to her seat.

Cole walked back too, squinting out the window as he put his food down on his table. "Would you . . . like to join me?"

With a forkful of eggs halfway to her mouth, she blinked up at him. "Really?"

He gestured at the seat opposite him. "Please."

She hesitated, gathered up her laptop, papers and purse and transferred everything to his table. Sitting down, eyeing him warily, she reminded him of that rabbit again.

The waitress, Carissa, came by with a steaming pot. "Coffee here, folks?" She poured two cups and dropped off a little silver jug of fresh cream. "Will this be . . . separate checks? Or . . ." she asked delicately.

"Yes, please—" Eden answered.

"No," Cole said simultaneously. "I've got this. I have a tab."

"That's very nice of you. Thank you."

"Seems the least I can do after barging in your room last night to ply you with alcohol."

"Seems like you got the worst of that," she deadpanned.

He forked some waffle and stuffed it in his mouth, then pointed at her with the utensil. "Well you're just full of Christmas cheer this morning."

"I'm just teasing. I have no idea anymore what you normally look like in the morning.

"For all I know, this could be it." She glanced up at him through her lashes, biting back a smile.

He shook his head and laughed.

"It's good to see you smile again," she said, breaking a piece of bacon in half before popping it in her mouth. "I was afraid there for a while that you never would."

"Were you now?"

"Mm-hmm," she mumbled. "Not that I'd blame you. But this is much nicer."

A mystery, this woman. He would never figure her out. They ate in awkward silence for a few minutes and he watched her surreptitiously, remembering how he used to love cooking for her in that tiny kitchen of his.

"What are your plans for today?" he asked finally, without calculating how that would sound. "It's going to be a beautiful day."

She looked out the window. "I thought . . . maybe I'd take the gondola up to the top. Take in the view while Quinn's in camp."

"Want some company?" he asked impulsively.

She looked surprised. Stunned, actually. "Um. Really? Well, sure. Do you want to come? I figured you'd be busy with lessons or something."

"Not for a little while yet. And I haven't gone up there for months. You know how it is. You live somewhere, and you forget it's a destination."

Finished eating, she placed her napkin down beside her plate. "Okay, then. I'll just drop my things off in my room and grab my coat. Meet you back in the lobby in fifteen?"

What the hell was he doing? "Okay. See you then."

"And, Cole? Thanks for breakfast. It was really good."

THE GONDOLA TO the top of the mountain originated at the center of the village where customers paid a decent amount of money to ride. But the ride operators were his employees and they waved him and Eden in without a ticket.

"You must be hooked up here," she said as they started up the mountain. "A regular table by the window, free gondola rides . . ."

"Jealous?" he asked, crooking one arm across the seat of the enclosed, four-man gondola.

"Maybe a little. Ooh, look at that."

She was staring out at the view of the lake in the distance. Deep, dark blue water bordered on turquoise in the morning sun where it lapped against the gigantic rocks on the half-frozen shoreline. He was watching the delight in her eyes. It reminded him he needed to look around this beautiful place more and not take it for granted. Such wonders were not part of most people's everyday lives, and he had been here so long he barely noticed it anymore.

The light hit her skin with a golden glow and turned her hair a paler shade of blonde. Never once had he forgotten how pretty she was. Not in eight long years. Yet seeing her again now, up close, smiling at his world, caught him off guard.

Giant spruce passed under their feet, soaring sixty feet high, but the gondola cleared them with a hundred feet to spare. It took nearly twenty minutes to reach the top, but they off-loaded onto a platform that curved around the snowy granite slabs of rock it perched upon. She asked him about the gondola, the crowd size, and even wondered out loud why more people weren't here to appreciate this spot.

"On a good summer day, there'd be a steady stream of tourists here. It's been a little slower this season. For the past couple of winters actually."

"I guess, because of the snow, right?" she asked. "Or lack thereof?"

"The drought really hit this area hard, but we're making a comeback."

She nodded.

"It's worth fighting for, this place," he said.

They strolled along the edge, watching the morning unfold across the valley below. "This should be a regular part of everyone's day. Everywhere," she said, smiling. "It's breathtaking."

"The Washoe people thought the lake was magical and dangerous. They were forbidden to swim in it. Because of Tessie, I guess."

"Tessie?"

"The local sea monster. This lake is so deep no one's ever really found the bottom. But the Washoe claimed that a giant bird lived in its depths somewhere and flew up to steal their people if they dared cross it in their canoes. Or if their children swam in it."

"Goodness. This Tessie . . . has anyone ever seen it?"

"Some have claimed to. And lived to tell the tale." He arched a brow.

She grinned. "This sounds like a campfire story that should be told in the dark."

"While making S'mores."

She giggled at the thought. "Just don't terrify Quinn. He'll never go in the water again. He already thinks there might be sharks in the pool. But, hey. We *should* roast marshmallows sometime. I've noticed the firepit at the resort."

"Every evening this week, complete with all the makings," he told her. "Part of the winter traditions at the Four Winds."

"I'm sure Quinn would love it if you'd join us. You could even tell him a tamer story than Tessie, if you want."

Join them? He'd be a fool to get more involved, but he found himself wanting to. She wasn't exactly pushing him away. That part of him that did not want to listen to reason found that fact . . . hopeful. "I guess that could be arranged," he said at last.

She cast a brilliant smile his way. "Okay then."

Below them, a family of deer made their way across the meadow between the trees. Eden took out her phone and captured the scene with a photo and she said she regretted that Quinn wasn't here to see this. Then she turned the camera on him.

At first, he shied away from having his picture taken. But she was insistent, so he let her. When she'd finished, she studied the shot for a long moment before deciding she was satisfied. Then he took out his own phone and did the same to her.

The light captured her beauty and the smile that made his gut clench. Not in the way he would have imagined twelve hours ago, but with an altogether different sort of ache. Damn if being here with her didn't feel right. They'd lost years but in a weird way, they could almost pick up where they'd left off. As if the way he'd wanted her once wasn't precisely the same as he did now—with his whole being, drawn to her like the incoming tide to the shore.

Eden approved of the photo he took, but said, "All well and good, but now we're just two people alone on a mountain."

An older woman nearby, bundled in a red wool coat and stylish hat, overheard this and said, "Here, you two stand over there. I'll take a picture with both of you in it."

Their gazes met in an awkward pause, but Eden said, "That's so kind of you. Thank you." And she handed the woman her phone.

She snapped two or three shots of them and handed the phone back. "There you go. You're such a cute couple. You should always memorialize moments like this together. My dear husband of forty years passed this last spring, and now all I have left of him are my memories and the pictures we took together."

"I'm so sorry for your loss," Eden said.

Her soft blue eyes grew moist. "Oh, thank you, dear. But we had a good life. We traveled all over the world together and took photos everywhere we went. Europe. India. The Maldives. And of course, every state in the Union. Many times, at Christmas. That's why I'm here now. And someday, you'll look back on this day and remember the good times you had when you were young and everything still lay ahead of you."

He didn't correct her about them. Instead, he allowed her story about them to hover there between them as Eden's gaze glanced over him. Maybe eight years ago, if they'd stayed together, all of this would be different now. They'd be long married, maybe with a child of their own, and Quinn too. And they would have taken many photos, documenting their lives together.

"Would you like a picture too?" Cole asked, touched by her story.

"Only if you two will be in it with me," she said with a conspiratorial smile.

"A selfie it is, then," he said and the three of them stood against the rail and the magnificent backdrop of the lake and mountains and he snapped a shot.

Later, as they walked back to the hotel, remembering the sweetness of the old woman and the photographs they'd taken, Eden said, "Is your number still the same? I can text you the photos."

"You still have my number?" he asked, surprised. "It hasn't changed." She nodded. He thought of all the times he'd begun to dial her number and quit before he'd hit send. Many, many times in those first few months. But he'd never deleted her number either. He wasn't sure why. Maybe just to torture himself with the possibility of talking to her again one day. But until she'd showed up here, he wasn't sure that would ever happen.

"Good then," she said. "I've got to go pick up Quinn. And then he has another lesson this afternoon. Not with you, I guess. But maybe we'll see you at the fire pit tonight? We'll be there around six-fifteen."

He had tech prep for the concert all afternoon and probably into the evening. "I'll try to make it. I've got a lot going on, but I'll do my best to be there."

Disappointment flickered behind her eyes, but she covered it with a smile. "Right. Okay. Thanks for coming with me today. And for breakfast."

With a muscle in his jaw working, he nodded. It would be vastly inappropriate to kiss her this early in the day. Or at all, he warned himself.

She hesitated. "Okay. Well. See you, Cole."

"Eden—" he called after her as she was about to push through the hotel doors. She turned back with a too bright smile.

"If I don't make it tonight, it won't be because I didn't

want to. Just so you know."

Something like relief stole across her face and she finger waved goodbye, disappearing into the lobby.

He didn't make it.

Tied up with incoming musicians and roadies, he worked late into the night. But his mind wasn't on that work. It was at the fire-pit with Eden and her son. Making memories.

Chapter Four

AFTER QUINN'S SKI lesson the next morning, Eden met him at the bottom of the hill. Behind the Santa beard, though, the ski instructor who brought him down was definitely not Cole. He was a very handsome, very blond twenty-something with a killer smile. But he wasn't Cole. Disappointment sliced through her with an unexpectedly sharp edge and she found herself scanning the slope for him.

Alexander the Great's mom, Amy, was there, picking up her twin boys, Zack and Adam, who were huddled in serious laughter with Quinn on their way off the slope. Just the sight of them all together made Eden smile.

"I think the boys made friends," Amy said, as they started back to the lodge. She pulled off her knit cap, setting her brown curls free. "We're here until after the Christmas concert if Quinn wants to get together with the boys. They're always so restless here without their pals."

"I hear you. A concert? That sounds great," Eden replied. "I'm sure Quinn would love that."

"Maybe we can all go together. And we're in room 2140!" Amy said, with the universal "call me" hand signal and turned to catch up with her boys as they split up. Quinn headed toward Eden.

Eden waved after her, hesitant to call out her room number across the yard. "Okay!"

"Hey! How was your lesson?" she asked Quinn as they walked back to the lodge. "You made friends with Zack and Adam?"

"Yeah. They're funny."

"You . . . you didn't have Cole this morning as an instructor?"

"Only for half the lesson. Then Kip came. He was nice too, but not as funny as Cole."

"Cole left halfway through?" That didn't seem like him.

Quinn nodded, his cheeks rosy, and little balls of ice hung off his mittens. "I told him you thought magic was just a trick and he said, 'Oh, yeah? Is that how this got behind your ear?'" Quinn proudly pulled off his mitten and held up a gold coin. "It's a whole dollar. Right there behind my ear all the time."

Eden smiled and glanced up the snowy hill wondering where Cole had gotten to. "Is that so?"

"Uh-huh. Who's right then?"

"Excuse me?"

"I mean about magic. Who's right? You or him?"

Now there was a loaded question. "Magic is really . . . a point of view. Maybe we're both a little right," she hedged. "But of course, mostly me."

Her son grinned up at her. She wasn't fooling anyone, least of all him. "Can I buy some candy with my money?"

"Absolutely." She threw her arms around him in a hug. "Then, what should we do the rest of the day? Wait . . ." she said. "You just let me hug you."

He smirked against her arm, apparently resisting the urge to shrug her off, which he'd been doing a lot of lately.

"I think I'm feeling a little dizzy with success!"

Busted, he laughed. "That's 'cause we don't know anybody here."

"Hey. You're way too young to be a teenager, Bub."

"Well, you're too old to get married."

That stopped the hug in its tracks. She stood back and looked at him. "What?"

"He wants you to, doesn't he?"

"You mean Wesley? Where'd you hear that?"

"I heard you talking to Nicole on the phone." *Little pitchers have big ears,* as her mother used to say. "And anyway, he told me he was going to ask you."

"He *what*?" Her eye twitched. "When?"

Quinn shrugged. "That day after basketball practice. While you were getting the car."

More than two weeks ago. Which might explain Quinn's mood for the last couple of weeks. Had he been sworn to secrecy or—?

"Are you? Going to?"

She opened her mouth and closed it again. Around

them, skiers glided past, lost in their own conversations. They stood, almost invisibly it seemed, at the center of the crowd. "I-I don't . . . think so."

Quinn sighed and looked away. "Don't you just say yes or no?"

"That's right. But I haven't said either yet." She tried to gather her thoughts as they walked toward the hotel. "Because, it's you and me, Quinn. Always. First."

He seemed almost disappointed by her answer. "Then why didn't *you* tell me?"

"I—" She squeezed her eyes shut before kneeling in front of him. "Oh, Quinn. I didn't want to say anything until I'd thought about it. I didn't want you to be disappointed or upset. And especially not before I'd even had a chance to figure out how *I* feel about it. I'm sorry. I should have told you."

"Are you?" His dark brown eyes sparkled with moisture suddenly.

She brushed his cheek with the back of her finger. He'd talked about that many times over the years—wanting that completeness once he'd been old enough to notice his friends had two parents. Even without truly remembering his family, he missed what they must have been together. "I thought you wanted a whole family. A mom and a dad. Like your friends."

But he shook his head. "We are a whole family. You and me," he said, then added, "and a dog."

She exhaled a laugh. "They say the secret to success is persistence. But I suspect you already know that."

He grinned, shoving back whatever vulnerable feelings he'd accidentally revealed to her.

Ruffling his dark hair, she drew him up against her side. "Didn't you say something about candy? I hear there's a terrific shop in the lobby with jars chock full of Skittles and gummy worms and chocolate." They bumped playfully into each other as they walked. "Too old to get married . . ." she mumbled. "Exactly how old do you think I *am*?"

ON THE OTHER side of the hotel, Cole was tending to last minute scheduling calls from musicians and managers, coordinating with the hotel's lighting manager about the outdoor venue where the concert was to take place, and posting on Instagram and Twitter about the show, a campaign he'd begun weeks ago, which was safely outside the purview of his technology-challenged partner. Though Granger was aware he had a holiday concert planned, Cole hadn't told him the extent of the costs for the show or everything about the show itself. It was a gamble. A big gamble. And if it didn't work, if it didn't bring in the guests he hoped to garner, then they'd have no choice but to accept one of the offers Granger had on his desk. But a good turnout might possibly save them. A great turnout probably would.

But hope wouldn't get him where he needed to be. He needed results.

Stopping by the front desk, he waited for a young couple with two children to finish up before leaning into front desk clerk, Katie Melbock, a young woman who'd started here as an intern when she was in college and had worked her way up.

"Morning, Katie."

"Morning, Mr. Hagan," she said with a bright smile. "How are you today?"

"Just wondering how our books are looking for the weekend."

She pulled up reservations on the screen. "Well, just this morning, we've booked another thirty rooms. And sold another fifty-five tickets to the concert to outside purchasers who will not be staying with us." Guests were comped for tickets, an enticement to book a room. "We're at eighty-seven percent."

Heartened by those numbers, he clapped the countertop with his palm. "That's what I want to hear. How are they hearing about it? Word of mouth? Social media?"

"Mostly Instagram, I'm hearing. They seem to be excited about the concert lineup. Especially for Jason Tunney." Her blue eyes flashed with a smile. "Everyone's favorite country star."

The cherry on top of all the terrific bands and singers

who'd said "yes" to his proposal, was Jason, one of Granger's personal discoveries and a local boy who'd made good in Nashville a few years back. He'd been at the top of the pop-country charts for several years running. It was a coup to get him, and Cole would find a way to show him his heartfelt gratitude. Nearly all of the bands had discounted their fees to take part in this event in honor of Granger's contribution to their careers. If Granger was serious about retirement, the concert's timing could not have been better.

With only three days until the show, nothing could go wrong. Not with the bands or the weather, which—*good news/bad news*—from all the forecasts looked as if no snow would muck up the evening. Nor, on the other hand, would it powder the hill for the influx of guests he was expecting. But they had plenty of snow makers for the ski trails, and if they could just get through the holidays in the black, then the rest of the winter might just take care of itself.

His mind wasn't entirely on the show, or the snow, or even the guests that he had greeted along the way this morning. He'd gotten little sleep last night, in fact, thinking about Eden. She had seemed as wary as a cornered cat last night, and he supposed his attitude hadn't helped much.

As he walked across the lobby, he stopped to talk to a few guests, as he did often, to see that their visit was going well. From the other side of the room, he heard Tom Linderall's grand piano, a sound that always made him happy. He'd been playing here for as long as Cole could remember and was one of those people that Granger had helped, long ago, as a starving artist. No longer a young man, Tom had aged gracefully and was nearing retirement himself. His full head of silver hair was the envy of most of the men on the staff.

"Tom," he said, as he got closer. Tom looked up from the piano, but his rendition of "Little Drummer Boy" didn't miss a beat.

"Hey, Cole. How's it going?"

"So far so good. You all set with your music for the concert? I understand the kid's chorale from St. Vincent's will singing backup for you and Lucy Yarnell."

Tom chuckled. "That'd be Lucy Yarnell, with me on backup piano. And only because her piano player's in Fiji for the holiday."

"She's gonna love you, Tom."

As Tom wrapped up "Little Drummer Boy" several people in the lounge broke out in spontaneous applause and one of them, a boy of about twelve, came over and put a dollar in his tip jar. Tom thanked him and grinned at Cole. "I love my job."

Cole clapped him on the shoulder. "Feeling's mutual."

Back at his office, he grabbed his coat and Mack's leash and headed outside with the dog. The day was brilliant and sunny, without any of the wind of the last couple of days. Mack trotted happily in front of him, sniffing at every post and bush, greeting every other dog he saw with a tail-wag and an invitation to play. For a while, Cole threw the ball for him in the fenced off dog park the hotel guests used, Mack's official greeting post.

The mindless game did little to distract him from thoughts of Eden and her son. Against his will, he'd found himself watching for them all morning, searching through the crowds for a glimpse and wondering what they were up to. He'd lain awake late last night, staring at the photo they'd taken on the mountain, unable to stop thinking about her. Imagining her taste again. The sound of her voice. Her scent, something citrusy and fresh, pushing up against him even in the fresh mountain air. The curve of her lip when she smiled.

Yesterday might have been a mistake, but it was human nature, he supposed, to want to know. To maybe find closure. But now that he knew about Quinn, that she hadn't married and that he'd glimpsed something in her eyes that made him hope—even though knew better—his old caution had been stripped away. It all made him want her again.

God knew, for the first couple of years A.E., or after Eden, as he sometimes referred to it, he'd walled himself off. In truth, his heart had been bruised and needed time to heal. He didn't blame her for that. Seeing her yesterday with Quinn, maybe she'd been right to go her own way. An athlete for a husband was a risky bet. He had to give her that. He might well have been a risky bet. Until he wasn't.

In the years after she left, he'd dived into skiing and snowboarding, harder than before, into competition and into being the best at what he did. He'd spent the next few years proving to himself he was more than the dreamer she'd thought he was. What he'd achieved he'd done through hard work and—yeah—by dreaming it into reality. Whether she wanted to admit it or not, dreams had been part of her success, too.

Mack jumped up on him, jolting him out of his reverie. Cole had dropped the ball in the game and Mack was pushy when it came to fetch.

"What? Not paying enough attention to you?" He scrubbed the dog's fur with two hands. "Sorry, Bud, I'm a little distracted."

Mack cocked an ear at him.

"You don't know her," he said. "But you'd like her. And her kid."

Mack wagged his tail as if to confirm that.

He tossed the ball up a few feet and caught it, distracted. "Yeah, but, there's no chance. She's moved on with her life. So have I. *We*. We've moved on, right, Mackie?"

Mack whined and lay down, putting his head on his large paws.

Cole frowned and tossed the ball up again. "What? You think I'm a fool for not trying? Maybe. But she's only here for a couple of days and look what happened last time." He clutched his heart dramatically.

A mournful yawn escaped Mack, whose eyes were still on the ball.

"Right? But . . . if I don't, I never get another shot at her.

How can I just let her go?"

His gaze cruised over the crowds near the entrance and, as if his thoughts had produced her, he saw her walking beside Quinn near the big outdoor fire pit. The pair stopped for the hot apple cider the hotel provided for guests who wanted to warm themselves by the fire. He watched her laugh at something her son said, and his heart gave a rusty little lurch, reminding him how long it had been since a woman's laugh had made him feel . . . anything, really.

Over the years, when he wasn't putting all his energy into this place, he'd dated now and then. A few women. But nothing serious. He supposed he hadn't allowed anything serious to happen. That was on him. Maybe all of this was a way to let her go.

Or to help her find her way back to him.

He leaned down to leash Mack back up. It was only a hundred yards or so from here to the fire. Maybe he could catch up with her. "Okay, fine," he told Mack. "There they are. If they leave before we get over there, that's the universe telling me I should just let it go. But if they stay—"

A surprise gust of wind swirled through the tree above him, pushing snow down from the branches.

Cole had only paused for a moment to turn his face up toward the drifting flakes when, out of nowhere, a small, scruffy dog wearing a service vest tangled his leash up with Mack's.

"Oh Enoch, no!" cried the woman who held the leash.

Tail wagging, the little dog jumped up to sniff Mack's face.

Annoyed and distracted, Cole leaned over to disentangle their leashes, but Mack wasn't having any of it. He was more than happy to sniff this new source of entertainment. Where had the two of them come from? A moment ago, he was sure he was alone in the dog park.

"I am so very sorry," the older woman said, her southern drawl pronounced as she fought to disentangle her dog. Despite her age—fifty? Sixty?—the woman looked strong enough to take him and Mack both with a hand tied behind her back. But she wore a sheepish expression on her sweet, round face that belied that intention. The dogs' leashes wrapped around their legs until Cole and the woman collided, face-to-face.

"Enoch! Look at what you're doin', crazy. Guess I should've taken off his leash in the park, shouldn't I? There's me not payin' attention."

Cole had to laugh. "Here," he said, reaching down to unleash Mack. "I'll just unhook them."

But dogs kept moving, keeping Mack's collar just out of reach.

"Enoch, hold still now!"

"I got it," Cole said, glanced up to find Eden and Quinn getting ready to leave. Finally, he managed to release both dogs. Mack jumped free of the mess and woofed playfully as Cole caught Enoch and handed him to the woman.

"Here you go," he said, but not before Enoch gave him a

wet lick on his cheek.

"Manners, Enoch!" the woman scolded, though she seemed amused. "He's got some love for you an' your dog, now."

"Mack, here, likes everybody," he said, clipping Mack's leash back on. "So, don't worry about it. I, uh, hope you're both enjoying your stay here at the Four Winds?"

She smiled up at him. A radiant smile that forced his annoyance to leak away. "*Mais oui.* You do meet the most interesting folk here."

Truth. Prime example? Her. A little eccentric, with bright eyes that caught you like a headlight when she turned them on you. Like he ought to know her somehow. But he was sure he hadn't seen her around before.

Rearranging her fringy green wrap around her shoulders, she chuckled. "I always say to Enoch, I say, nothing ventured, nothing gained. So, it's his business to meet everyone. And Christmastime, after all, couldn't be a better time for makin' new friends. And renewing old acquaintances, I would wager."

Old acquaintances, indeed. He couldn't spot Eden at the fire pit, but there were a lot of people between them now. He tugged Mack toward him and started toward the gate.

"Better hurry," he heard the woman say.

He turned back. "What?"

"What?" Her chocolate-brown eyes were wide, her expression cluelessly amused.

He frowned. "I thought you—?"

She canted a look at him.

"Never mind."

"Well, then," she said. "We'll just be on our way then."

He nodded, giving her dog a pat on the head. "You and—"

"—Enoch."

"You and Enoch enjoy your day now."

"*Mais oui*, we will. We surely will," she said smiling. "You as well, Cole. *Au revoir*!"

But he was already heading out of the dog park to try to find Eden. Somehow, over the course of a few minutes, finding her had gone from a maybe to a must. But he couldn't see her anywhere now. Glancing through the glass doors as he reached them, he searched the lobby area and saw no sign of her there either.

He stopped at the fire pit, turning in all directions, but she was gone. So much for fate helping him out. He frowned. Even the old woman at the dog park had vanished. Strange bird. And . . . wait . . . had she just called him by name?

You as well, Cole. Au revoir!

What the—? He couldn't remember telling her his name. Mack leaned against his leg and Cole reached down to pet him, absently plucking a few stray white feathers from his coat. He turned one between his fingers, staring at it.

"Hot cider for you, Mr. Hagan?"

Barry Stern, the holiday intern from a nearby college and son of a longtime employee in accounting, stood a few feet away, holding out a steaming insulated paper cup to him. His cheeks bore slashes of red from the cold and his curly dark hair was nearly hidden under a wool cap.

"Sorry. What?"

Barry scratched Mack behind the ears. "I just thought maybe you came over for a cup. You okay? You lose something?"

He tossed the feather and jammed his hands in his pockets. Eden was nowhere. Gone. "Hard to say, actually," he answered. *If you never had something in the first place, could you actually lose it?*

That's when his fingers encountered something foreign and hard at the bottom of his pocket and he pulled it out. What the—?

It was a small, silver top hat. A game piece. The kind you'd find in Monopoly—a game he hadn't played in years. How had *that* found its way into his pocket?

"Here. Have some cider," Barry urged. "I've gotta look like I'm working when the boss comes by."

Cole curled his fist around the top hat, shoved it back in his pocket, and accepted the cider. "I don't think you need to worry."

"Hey. I was lucky enough to get the night off for the concert coming up. I'm bringing my girlfriend and some other friends from school. There's a buzz building about it over there."

Buzz was good. He needed that in a big way to make this event happen. Only at that moment did it occur to him that he might be going to that concert alone. He chugged the apple cider and tossed the cup in the trash. But he'd be too busy, as usual, for that to matter. "That's great. Keep up the good work."

He turned and ran straight into—

"*Ooof!*"

"Whoa! Eden!" Steadying her by the shoulders, he held her away from him. "Sorry. Are you okay?"

Frowning at their point of collision—his chest—she delicately fingered her injured nose. "Maybe?" She tapped his chest with her mittened hand. "I think you've been working out."

He just laughed. She did too, for the first time, really, since he'd seen her. The sound rocked through him like lightning in a bottle. God, he'd missed her laugh.

"We were just out here a minute ago," she told him, glancing around at the area, "and Quinn forgot his gloves on—" Barry, overhearing, produced them STAT "—the bench. Ah!" Blushing, she held them up to Cole as proof and thanked Barry.

Quinn, who had followed her out the door, immediately dropped down in front of Mack to pet him. "Is *this* your dog?"

"Yep. This is McConnell's Pride himself. Mack for

short."

Mack dropped the ever-present gooey tennis ball in his mouth and gave Quinn a slobbery kiss, eliciting a delighted giggle from the boy.

Cole and Eden both spoke at once.

"I'm glad—"

Eden started over. "I-I'm so glad we ran into you. I was hoping we would."

"Me too," he said.

"You were? I mean, I thought after last night—"

"I got hung up at—"

"No, I got your text. Thanks. And no worries," she said, holding up her hand. He guessed she'd already written him off as not interested.

"How about I make it up to you tonight? The two of you. Six o'clock?"

"Oh. Well . . . I . . ."

At her hesitation, he added, "Not a date."

"Oh. Right. No."

"Just a friendly guided tour?" At a loss for a better word for what he had in mind, he fell silent.

"That sounds great," she said. "Doesn't it, Quinn?"

Quinn nodded, busy petting Mack and stroking his paw.

Cole went on, "There's a lot going on for the holidays, and I happen to know all the secret handshakes. What kind of a friend would I be if I let you two navigate it all alone?"

That sexy mouth of hers widened into a smile. "We

could hardly turn an offer like that down."

"Can Mack come?" Quinn asked.

Hearing his name, Mack sat at attention, wagging his tail against the snow.

"I mean," Cole quipped, "do reindeer fly?"

Quinn giggled. "No!"

Eden bit her lips at Cole.

"Oh, yeah, I forgot, you don't believe in flying reindeer either. We're gonna have to work on that." He flicked a look at her, and she arched a brow at him. "Mack's generally my shadow, unless I'm skiing. He's not particularly fond of the chair lift. So, yeah. He can come." He checked his watch. "Listen, I've got some things to tie up, but I think I know something you two might like later if you want to meet up."

The arguments against it flittered across her expression then vanished. "Okay," she said. "Where should we meet?"

"In the lobby by the gingerbread house." The giant, fully decorated gingerbread house that had every child in the hotel *ooh-ing* and *ahh-ing* as they walked through the lobby.

She nodded. "We'll be there."

"Don't eat first. I know a place where the burgers are off the charts good. Unless you don't like burgers, Quinn."

The kid laughed as if that idea couldn't be more ridiculous. Eden sent him a helpless grin. Seeing her smile up at him again after all these years was like a door opening inside him. One that had been closed for a long time. Maybe the universe was on his side after all. Or, at least, it was trying to give him a shot. The rest was up to him.

"So, we'll see you at six?" Eden said.

"Dress warm," he said before heading back toward his office with Mack at his heels. "But that's the only hint you're getting."

A slow smile worked its way across his face.

Chapter Five

THAT AFTERNOON, EDEN put Quinn in the hotel kids camp for a couple of hours while she did some reconnaissance on the hotel. It was a beautiful place, really, and aside from the sad state of the snowpack, she couldn't understand why the hotel wasn't fully booked up for the holidays. She spoke informally with a few employees, ascribing her questions to curiosity, which they were happy to answer. She couldn't find a complaint about the management or the pay or even the hours, though several mentioned that the hotel had only taken on a fraction of the seasonal staff this year as compared to other years. And the rest were making up the difference in hours.

She'd walked down into "the village" shops that were attached to the hotel and prowled through them, asking questions there too. Several shops had signs announcing "store closing" sales and when she asked, a few admitted that the last few seasons had been hard and several shops had already closed. They also added that Mr. Stuart and his partner had been doing what they could to support the struggling shops.

"This place, working here has been like family," one shop owner told her as she cleaned the glass countertop near her register. "It'll be a great loss to leave it behind."

Eden bought a hand-painted scarf from the woman and a snow globe for Quinn before wandering down the walkway back to the hotel. If there was a unifying theme to her research this morning, it was that this place was more than a job for most who worked here. It was like their reason for coming to work every day, their reason for smiling. It was the inflection point for many of their lives, the thing that had made a difference for them.

As she walked, she allowed herself to ponder what would become of all of it after her company was finished with it. Certainly, they meant to keep the resort running, improve it, find ways to make it more successful. But like all big, corporate ventures, something valuable would be lost. That thing that had taken a whole generation to build would become nothing more than a corporate machine, churning out five-star service from a rotating influx of workers.

Though, none of that was really her concern. It was her job. She was strictly advising and observing this week. But the thought of what the transfer of this place would mean to all these people, including Cole, made her feel unexpectedly nauseous.

She bought herself a coffee and sat down at an outdoor table on the walkway just as her cell phone rang.

Wesley.

He'd called twice already, and she knew she had to talk to him.

"Hi!" she answered brightly.

"Hi yourself," Wesley said, sounding confused. "Where've you been? I've called a couple of times."

"I'm so sorry. Quinn has kept me very busy since we got here. I just haven't had a minute to call you back." That was an ugly lie, and she hated herself for telling it.

"If I didn't know better, I'd think you were avoiding me." She could picture the hurt look on his handsome face. And, how, sometimes, he used that look to make her change her mind about something or other.

She brushed at the chill on her cheek with the backs of her fingers. "What? No! Not at all. How are things at the office?"

Was he counting to ten? "The office is fine. But that's not why I'm calling."

"Right, but just so you know, I've just been prowling around this place all afternoon talking to people and—"

"Eden. Babe. Slow down. It's just us. You and me. What's goin' on?"

"Going on? Nothing." Cole, smiling, handing her a glass of wine, tumbled through her memory. "What do you mean?"

"I mean," he said slowly, "you're dancing as fast as you can around the elephant in the room. It's right there. Big and platinum and inside a blue Tiffany box."

She fell silent for so long he said, "Eden? You there?"

"I'm still here. Listen . . . Wesley . . ."

He growled. "I don't like the sound of that."

"My life is complicated, you know? With Quinn and my job."

"And I'm trying to un-complicate it."

"Nothing about marriage is uncomplicated. You know that."

"You're worried about Quinn. I get it."

"Of course, I am." He was the most important person in her life. And the change she'd seen in him just since coming to the mountains made her want to take a step back from everything, including the idea of marrying Wesley.

"Hey, Quinn and I will work it out," he said. "He may not like me much now, but it won't always be that way."

"How do you know?"

"Kids grow up. They get lives of their own. Friends. He won't be so dependent on you forever."

"You can't just wait out a kid's childhood until he gets over needing you. Hoping that he'll turn out okay. He's seven, Wesley. Seven years old. Of course, he's dependent on me. He's supposed to be. I'm his mother."

"Maybe it's you who's too dependent on him."

Excuse me? "What?"

"You know what I mean."

"No. I don't think I do."

"I don't want to fight here, Eden."

"Maybe you do. Maybe we are." She could hear him breathing on the other end of the line. Exhaling in frustration was more accurate. Feeling the same, she got to her feet and stalked down the cobblestone street toward the hotel, tossing her coffee in the nearest trash can. "Maybe we shouldn't be talking about marriage yet at all. Maybe—"

"—maybe you're using him as an excuse because you're afraid to do what's right for you. Or maybe you just want to prove you don't need anyone, including me."

That stung. "That's . . . that's not fair. And not true."

"Yeah. Well, what do I know?" he said. "I'm just stabbing in the dark here, trying to guess what you're thinking because you never tell me. Trying to figure out why you'd turn me down when we make such a good team."

"Being a 'good team' is not exactly a compelling reason to get married, Wesley."

"Eden. I want to marry you. I want to go to bed with you at night and wake up with you in the morning. Have coffee on our deck and share our days and everything else. I love you. Okay? Is that what you need to hear?" *Did she?* "But if you want daisy chains and kumbaya around the campfire, that's not me. I am who I am. And I'm not that guy who's going to read you poetry from a little book or . . . or give up steaks or whatever to prove how 'woke' I am. But you're not that either. I know you. You're a practical, no BS kind of woman. You know who you are and what you want. And you're exactly who I want."

"You . . . want to marry me because . . . I'm practical?" Good Lord. She had made this particular bed with her own two hands. She had no one to blame but herself.

"We're good together is what I'm saying," he went on. "And aside from the obvious—the fact that I'm crazy about you—look at us. We're unstoppable. You and I have almost single-handedly turned this company around."

She definitely wouldn't go that far—

"—so why would you walk away from that?"

Eden froze. *Walk away*? From what? Her job? The cold air outside slid between the seams of her coat. "What . . . what's that supposed to mean?"

He blew out an exasperated breath. "I meant walk away from me. Okay? Damn, Eden. I can see that we're not going to get anywhere talking about this now."

She pictured him pacing around his office like a caged cat. She'd seen him do this many times through his glass office walls, leaning into his phone to make a point. So often, over the past years, she'd found that part of him attractive. That never-give-up spirit. That almost ruthless part of him that wouldn't tolerate losing. Now, directed at her, pushing her for a choice she wasn't ready to make, she found that intensity intimidating. But he was right. They shouldn't talk about this now.

"When are you coming home?" he asked, breaking into her thoughts.

She contemplated saying never. "Um . . ."

"Will you at least be home for Christmas?"

"There's a Christmas concert coming in a few days here that I'd like to stay for. A promotion the hotel is putting on. Jason Tunney is appearing, and he's a big draw. Quinn would like to see him too. And there are more people to talk to here. I haven't made inroads with management yet, but I'm going to try. As far as Christmas goes . . . I don't know yet."

"A concert? Okay. You do what you need to do. I'll be here when you get back. And we'll work this out. We are going to work this out."

That sounded suspiciously like a mandate. She nodded at the cobblestones and said goodbye.

As she walked toward the hotel, she passed crowds of families heading to the slopes, laughing, or agreeing on meet-up times. Mothers, fathers, kids. She pulled her gaze to the mountain where skiers were plummeting down the trails with abandon. Some traversed the trails in careful zig-zags, avoiding the moguls and the dive-bombing snowboarders. Some stood still, enjoying the view. It occurred to her that for years—since Quinn, at least—her life had moved so fast, she'd fallen into survivor mode, her long-ago list of goals she'd once thought so important were now a confused jumble she couldn't be certain she even wanted anymore. She'd changed.

Wesley was still stuck on the old her. The her before Quinn. That ambitious girl who had put her life on hold to do what needed doing to succeed. He liked that about her. Maybe even loved that. But that other part of her, the part that Quinn had uncovered as he'd snuck into her heart, maybe that was not part of the bargain with Wesley, and Quinn was just a distraction.

What was right for her could only be what was *also* right for her son. She was responsible to make sure her son's life turned out every bit as brilliant as it would have if Jo and Aaron had survived. Did she need him? Yes. As he needed her. Did that mean she was pushing Wesley away? Maybe.

If she'd learned one thing as a parent, it was that kids were brilliant at uncovering things. They were like little x-ray machines who could look through any façade you held up to them. Or like dogs with a sixth sense about people and love, and right where to find them.

She reached the lobby and had her hand on the glass door when she looked up to see her friend from work, Nicole Jessup, walking away from the fire pit. Her burgundy sweater, jeans, and light jacket were no match for the cold breeze cutting across the mountain, which curtained her blonde hair across her face. And her stiletto heeled black boots were treacherous and fabulous, as always, but sinking into the snow. Lifting her hair away from her face, she grinned broadly when she saw Eden.

"*What*?" Eden cried.

"Surprise!" Nicole laughed and opened her arms, which Eden walked right into. "Hey. I figured you might need a hug."

"Oh. My. God. You are crazy. Did you just hop on a plane from LA?"

She grinned. "Kind of. I flew into Reno and rented a car to drive to my mom's place in Carson City for Christmas, and I thought I'd stop by on my way to see if you were all right. I can't believe I found you out here. I was just about to storm the hotel."

Eden laughed. "Only you would do that." She hugged her again. "How long are you here for?"

"Just the afternoon. I promised Mom I'd be there tonight."

"Well, you are just in the nick of time to save me from myself. Or . . . something like that."

"That sounds dire. And intriguing. And like I totally should have come. What's going on?"

"This convo," she said, threading her arm though Nicole's as they headed to the lobby, "requires a hot toddy by the roaring fire. Besides, I've been out here for a while and I'm freezing."

Nicole shivered, tugging the sides of her too-thin jacket together. "My thoughts exactly. And look at this place. It's Christmas everywhere." Indeed, the entire street was one big advertisement for Christmas. They walked under decorated boughs hanging from lampposts. Nearby, a cute couple was kissing under a bunch of mistletoe dangling from a signpost.

Side-eyeing them, Eden admitted, "All the holiday cheer

is either growing on me, or I'm having a breakdown. Either way, it's a bit contagious." In her own defense, she pulled the snow globe she'd bought for Quinn out of her bag and gave it a shake. Snow swirled around a tiny Santa carrying a bag of toys.

"Okay, where is the real Eden Kendall and what have you done with her?"

Eden laughed. "That *is* the question. Nicole, do you believe in magic?"

"Magic? You mean like David Copperfield? Penn and Teller?"

"I mean the life-altering kind where fate steps in and throws you a curveball, but you have a feeling it's no curveball at all?"

"Oh, this *is* serious. Tell me everything."

EDEN WATCHED NICOLE stare into the flickering fire burning in the giant stone fireplace at the center of the common cocktail area, contemplating what Eden had just told her. About Cole. About Wesley. About the shifting snow underneath her feet.

"So, you're the one who broke his heart. And yet, still . . . ?"

"Still," she agreed. "I'm not sure why he asked me out tonight. I don't know why he's even forgiven me."

"You sure he has?"

"No. I guess that remains to be seen." She dropped her head in her hands. "My question is, what am I doing?"

"Exploring your options?" Nicole said, sipping her Irish coffee. "Let me ask you this. It's been eight years. How do you feel about him?"

"I was in crazy in love with him then. And yet, I let my head rule my heart. I think I never got over him, even though I was the one to walk away. He was funny and optimistic and smart and way too much like my parents. A dreamer, like my father. My father's a musician, a prop man, a jack of all trades who was always waiting for his big moment to arrive. It's not that he didn't hard work for it. He did. But it never really happened for him. He wrote commercial jingles for a while and my mother taught art until the art budgets in the schools dried up. And then she just had crappy jobs to pay the rent. My dad, too. We moved a lot. He gave up music finally. He was artistic in so many different directions he never focused on one thing. Which left him disconnected from all the things."

"So they struggled financially," Nicole said.

Eden nodded. "And they loved me through every minute of it. They even loved Cole, even though he was doomed to repeat their lives with his skiing dreams. Impractical, right? But that's why I love them so much. They have always supported what I wanted. Even this job, though they privately hoped I'd find something to bring me joy." She laughed.

"Their guiding principle."

"And?"

"And I did. In a backward, awful way. I have Quinn."

Nicole nodded. "And Cole?"

Eden exchanged looks with her. "He made me feel like I could do anything. He taught me to ski even though I was afraid. He skied backward all the way down the hill that first day when I literally kept falling every ten feet or so. He wouldn't let me quit. But he never left my side. The snowplows were coming up the hill and the sun had set before I made it down to the lodge." She laughed, remembering. "And then, he roasted me a marshmallow and told me he loved me. I know that's a silly little thing, but I've always remembered how he made me feel."

"How long did you two date?"

"Two years. One month. Six days."

"Oh, boy." Nicole shook her head with a grin. "Girl, you don't remember those kinds of things unless you never got over him."

"Right," she said with a sigh. "I suppose that's true. We dated in college. Seriously dated. Sometimes, we'd just stay in and watch movies together. And he would let me draw him. Because . . . that face."

"You draw?"

She nodded. "Used to. Not anymore."

"Go on," Nicole prodded.

"I would draw him, and he would cook for me. And

we'd do the *New York Times* crossword puzzle together. And he always knew the words. He was smart, but a jock at the same time. He wanted to marry me. But in our senior year, he got a minor sponsorship from a skiwear company, and he needed to go and ski full-time. Quit school. He wanted me to come with him. And I couldn't. I had a scholarship. He said he'd wait for me. And I told him—I told him not to. I broke up with him. And I broke his heart."

"Why did you break it off? Fear?"

"Fear of repeating my parent's life? Yeah. The instability? Living paycheck to paycheck. I think I decided when I was young that I wouldn't do that lifestyle. Couldn't. I mean, for me, yeah, I wanted not to worry about tomorrow like I had my whole life. But it was really for them, for my parents. I felt . . . responsible. That sounds crazy right? But I knew what would happen to them. I could see it coming. It was already there. I couldn't leave them without a net. And I was *it*. Just me. They gave me everything they could. Everything I am. And I owed them that.

"Now," she went on, "they're okay. It's not as dire as it could have been. They're happy and getting by. I do help them now and then because I can. So, I know it sounded selfish and wrong to leave Cole the way I did. And dumb on the surface. But I didn't see a choice back then. I needed security checked off my list and back then, he didn't even *have* a list."

"By all accounts," Nicole said, "you're successful."

"Am I? At my job, maybe. But I'm in a relationship that's more convenient than passionate and here I am, still contemplating the one that got away."

"Catch and release," she pointed out.

"Right. It would be so much easier if I . . . if I loved Wesley. If I had never loved Cole."

Nicole sat back, sipping her drink. "You don't mean that."

Eden squinted at her. "I don't know what I mean right now."

"Listen, to everything there is a season. It might have been Cole's season then, but, for many reasons, it wasn't yours. Your timing was off. It happens."

"What's changed?"

"You have," Nicole pointed out. "You're not your parents. We only get this one shot at life. At happiness."

"Maybe I've already had it. Maybe we're just bad for each other."

"And maybe not."

Eden shook her head. "Tonight is just a mystery outing. With my son. He's just being friendly. It's probably nothing."

"Or it's something."

"Does wanting to go make me a horrible person? I mean, I haven't even told Wesley no."

"And you haven't said yes," Nicole reminded her. "And that proposal was all his doing, not yours. It doesn't obligate you to say yes."

"It's not that simple. If I say no . . ." She leaned her head back in the tall, wingback chair that sat near the fire. "My job . . . might actually go away. Fade to nothing. Seven years of work. Only to start all over again."

"You can't marry him because of your job," Nicole said. "Can you?"

She sighed. "Of course not. But it's not irrelevant. Wesley and I, we've had fun together. We work well together. But I'm not in love with him. And he doesn't want a kid. He doesn't want to be a parent. He wants me, but not the responsibility of Quinn. That's obvious. And that is a hard no. I'm an idiot for hoping it could all turn out all right."

"No. You're human. You're a woman. And you're in a pickle."

"Of my own making," Eden admitted. "So, I shouldn't go out with Cole?"

"You absolutely *should* go out with him. Go. See what happens. This might be your last chance. And if nothing comes of it, then you'll know. And you won't always wonder 'what if?'"

"He doesn't know what I do, what I'm doing here. And if I tell him, well, that might just end things right there. I'll put him out of work. He's a ski instructor. He needs this job. He probably lives paycheck to paycheck."

"You'll have to figure that out. I'm pretty clear how John Russell and Wesley would feel about you outing yourself here while you're on their dime. But in the end, that's something you'll have to weigh."

"My scale seems to be *very* unreliable these days," Eden said.

Nicole chuckled. "My mother always said it was just as easy to fall in love with a rich man as a poor man. I say you fall in love with the one you're meant to be with. Maybe this is just the universe giving you the push you need to find that life for yourself. Whether it's with Cole or someone else." She hesitated, then went on. "I'm just going to say this because I think you need to hear it before you make your decision."

How cryptic. Eden felt cold creep up her spine. "What are you talking about?"

Nicole swallowed hard. "Here goes. Please don't hate me for telling you this. But as the company has gotten larger, and Wesley has taken on more responsibility from his father, he's literally begun working behind the scenes, sabotaging the companies Wildwood is trying to acquire. An insurance policy for acquisition, if you will. Companies that are struggling. I've seen them do it. I've seen the paperwork."

Taken aback, Eden shook her head. "Sabotaging? What do you mean?"

"I mean using Wesley is using his connections to bury them. By whatever means possible. Wooing away suppliers. Planting doubts with capital supporters. You remember that Savannah resort deal last year? The trucking company debacle?"

She blinked. "Leaving the resort scrambling for clean linens for the holiday weekend?"

"Wesley managed that fiasco, and it was the death knell for them. He's got a ruthless edge, Eden. He doesn't play fair. Please tell me you didn't know this."

"I didn't. But how . . . how could I *not* know that? We work together. On everything."

"He's kept it from you. Intentionally. Not just you. There's only one other person in the company who knows what they're up to besides the people who are doing the interfering. It was Monica who told me. She said it was Wesley who talked his father into implementing this tactic as good business."

Monica—as in Wesley's assistant. *And Monica would know.* So why hadn't she herself known? She had long suspected other companies of doing this sort of thing, but Wildwood Acquisitions had a reputation for honesty and fairness. It was one of the main reasons she had gone to work for them. Now this . . .this changed everything. But he'd done this under her very nose.

She felt suddenly ill. As if everything Wesley had ever told her was a lie. What an idiot she'd been.

She took Nicole's hand.

"You okay?" her friend asked.

Eden nodded. In fact, she felt almost liberated, if that made any sense at all. On the other hand, everything she thought she knew had just shifted underneath her. Eden swallowed hard, staring at the fire. "Thank you for telling me."

"I'm sorry."

"I'm not. It makes everything clearer suddenly."

"Well, that leads me to my next bit of news. Connected news."

"Oh, no. What?"

"I wanted to tell you first. I was offered a new job."

Eden's eyes widened. "At Wildwood?"

"No. It's a non-profit in Santa Barbara working on ridding the ocean of plastics. It's a great job, and a friend of mine recommended me for it. I spoke to them yesterday and they offered me the job. It's good money, a good cause. Something I can feel good about doing."

"You're taking it." Eden could tell by the look on her face.

Nicole nodded. "It's time. For me anyway. Wildwood's been good to me, but I need a change. I'll miss you so much."

Eden shook her head with a bright smile. But inside, she felt like crying. Without Nicole there, working at Wildwood Acquisitions wouldn't be the same. But knowing what she knew now, it wasn't even clear she could keep working there. Not to mention the mistake she'd made with Wesley. What a mess she'd made of everything. But she tried for brightness as she said, "Congratulations. I'm happy for you. When do you go? Does anyone else know?"

"After the fifteenth of January and no, I'll give my notice after I get back. No reason to spoil anyone's holiday. Except yours, of course. Sorry."

Eden hugged her again. "Well, except for that news, I'm so glad you came today."

"Me too. Now, I must see Quinny before I go. Let's go find him. I want to say hi to him before I go."

After Nicole left, Eden spent an hour trying on every outfit in her suitcase, initially discarding them all. She finally settled on a simple green, cowl-neck sweater and black jeans for their "date" with Cole. *Nice without trying too hard.* Except that she remembered green was the color she wore the first time he'd said he loved her, that night at the local pizza dive. And ever after, pepperoni and beer reminded her of him. But he wouldn't remember that sweater. She could hardly remember that girl.

Quinn peppered her with questions about where they were going tonight, rolling his eyes when she changed her hairstyle three times before giving up on style and settling on a messy bun.

"You look nice, Mom," Quinn told her as they took the elevator downstairs.

She wanted to kiss him. "You look pretty nice yourself."

"Do you like him? Cole, I mean?"

"Sure. I do," she said truthfully. "We're friends from a long time ago."

"I think he likes you."

She side-eyed her son.

"No, really, I think he likes you."

She didn't want to get her hopes up. She felt flustered and a little nauseous and scared that she would say the wrong thing. She wasn't even sure what she was hoping for out of this "non-date," but she decided to have faith that whatever would come of tonight was what should happen.

They met Cole at six and ate burgers at a hopping burger joint in the village where Quinn revealed his prowess for consuming every boys' favorite meal—including all of her French fries. They talked about nothing and everything, but mostly about Quinn and what he was up to in his life. She felt all the warm fuzzies as she watched the two of them interact, with Quinn being uncharacteristically open with Cole about things he rarely discussed, even with her. The reticence that was always evident with Wesley was nowhere to be seen.

She wondered briefly if that was only because Quinn knew this was nothing permanent and it felt safe to befriend Cole, where it hadn't been with Wesley. But just as quickly, she dismissed that theory, hearing Quinn laugh with Cole and respond to his playful personality. No, they were two different men, Cole and Wesley, and Quinn made it very clear which one he preferred.

AFTER DINNER, THEY'D strolled through the village with Mack, who'd waited patiently in Cole's car for them as they ate dinner. Now, he ran playfully alongside them.

"Can I hold his leash?" Quinn asked, standing as close to the dog as he could get.

"Sure. Keep your eye on him, though. He loves to run."

Quinn just laughed and ran ahead of them on the snowy path near the hotel, scooping up snow as he went. Mack ran along beside her son, playfully woofing and kicking up snow.

He and Eden walked behind, watching the boy and the dog play. For just an instant, Cole imagined what it might have been like if they'd never broken up. If that little boy running ahead had been theirs to raise together. A useless, out-there thought he would do well to put away in a corner somewhere.

He glanced over at her and caught her watching him. She blushed and looked away, but not before he'd glimpsed something she probably hadn't wanted him to see. Wistfulness? He wondered if their thoughts had, at that moment, run along the same line.

As they walked, she said, "Thanks for dinner. That was nice of you to think of Quinn."

"My pleasure. He's a great kid. Easy to spend time with."

"I think so," she said, "but I'm his mom. He talks about you all the time, you know. I've never seen him take to someone like he has taken to you."

"Yeah? Maybe it's just my dog."

"Maybe." She chuckled. "Unfortunately, I work too much to have time for one."

"What is it exactly you do these days? Still painting?"

She seemed surprised he remembered. "Not anymore. Not for a long time."

"You were so good."

Her art, he'd always supposed, had been a spillover from her parents' love of all things artistic, but another one of those things she'd pushed away. Like him.

"You were always my biggest—make that *only*—fan. Deluded though you were. No, art was never going to get me where I wanted to go."

Amused, he shook his head. "Not everything we love is practical."

"True. Just ask my parents."

Ironically, her parents had been some of his favorite people. Free-spirited, always laughing . . . they both ate up life. The same way Eden herself had once been before giving up on all the things that didn't fit into her vision for her future.

"So, what pays the bills now?" he asked. "You never told me what you do."

"Oh," she said, adjusting her scarf around her neck. "Uh . . . basically, I work in . . . real estate development."

"On your own? Or . . .?"

"A company. I work for a company." She made a point of not meeting his eye as she laughed. "Not very interesting."

"I'm interested. Residential or—?"

"Commercial. You've never heard of them. Believe me. By the way"—she craned a look back at the hotel, which was disappearing behind them—"where exactly are we going?"

"Just ahead. See those lights?"

Up ahead, a swarm of lanterns hung from the trees, flickering beneath snow-covered pine boughs. Under those, a few people waited in line beside several horse-drawn sleighs. The impatient animals exhaled steamy breaths into the cold night air. A pair of wranglers tended to the draft horses as guests clambered onto the hay-covered flatbed sleigh standing beside the two classic four seat sleighs.

Chapter Six

EDEN TURNED A surprised look back at him. "No way! You have tickets?"

He held up two hands. "Did you doubt me?"

"Oh, Cole. No, but, a sleigh ride? I tried to get us in the first day we got here. They were all booked up for the rest of the holiday. How did you manage it?"

"I told you, I'm hooked up here." He whistled to Mack, who came bounding back to them, tugging Quinn along behind.

"Mom, Adam and Zack are up there too. They even have Alexander the Great with them. Can I ride with them?"

"Well, I don't know. Cole's got tickets for—"

"—I'm sure they can squeeze you in on the hayride," he said. "We're all going to the same destination. Eden, you and I can take the sleigh and meet him there."

Quinn squealed and did a little celebratory dance.

"Let me talk to Amy first," Eden began, but the twins' mother was already waving to her and beckoning Quinn to the wagon.

"We'll meet you at the other end!" Amy shouted, tugging

on Alex's leash.

Eden waved at her, agreeing.

"Yo, Mr. Hagan!" said called one of the two sleigh drivers. "We're all set."

Cole sent him a nod and flicked a look at Eden, who was smiling curiously at him. "*Mister* Hagan? Wow. I guess you are hooked up."

"Told ya." He guided her toward the empty sleigh that would carry the two of them and Mack.

He helped her aboard and tucked a thick, furry blanket around them as they settled in for the ride. Mack wedged himself on the floor between their knees, happy as an otter in snow. Eden waved to Quinn, but he was too busy laughing with the other boys as the hay wagon started down a luminary-lit path into the woods.

With the crescent moon hanging in the dark, cloud-scudded sky, the brown-bag luminaries, lit from within by candles, guided their path down the wide, winding trail. It was a magical world out here at night, with the dark wrapping around them in the wilderness. The rhythm of the horses' hoof beats, muffled by the snow, rocked them gently and the bells on their harnesses were like music in the night air.

"It's beautiful," she murmured.

"One of my favorite things," he admitted. "I haven't done this in a long time."

"Too busy skiing?"

"Something like that."

"If I lived here, I'd do this every night. Until I ran out of money." She sighed. "But I guess there are a lot of things I've gotten too busy for. Coming here has been good for us. For me and Quinn. He needed this as much as I did."

Mack tipped his big, broad head back against Eden's knee, asking for a rub. She obliged. "He's a beauty. How long have you had him?"

"He was just a pup when I found him. He was up on the mountain, chest deep in snow. I don't know how he got there, or how long he'd been there before I found him. He was practically a pup-cicle. Weren't you, boy? I picked him up, tucked him in my arms and skied down the hill with him. We've been together ever since. My luck. Their loss, whoever did that to him."

She shook her head, stroking the dog. "Life is funny, how it works, isn't it? That you happened down that particular path that day."

He was staring at her now. "Yeah. It is."

The sleigh glided along the luminary-lit path with the occasional lantern in a tree that provided just enough light to make their way. The big draft horses seemed to know the way by heart anyway, and the gentle rocking of the sleigh was soothing and made her relax against the back of the seat. Against Cole's arm.

As she did, she felt his hand cup her shoulder for a moment, almost as an instinct, before backing off. It was a touch so familiar yet so distant she almost pulled his hand back around her again. But she didn't. Instead, she looked over at him in time to catch him smiling at her.

That easy smile of his sent a rush of longing through her. For what, exactly she couldn't say. Connection? A kiss? That feeling of belonging that she'd walked away from so many years ago? That ease they had together that had nothing to do with ambition or her career? It all seemed odd now that she had some perspective—now that she had Quinn—that she'd been foolish enough to think she'd ever find someone like him again. In her naiveté, she'd imagined greener pastures somewhere up the road. Pastures lush with security and reason. A self-supporting career she could manage on her own. Well, she'd nearly achieved that small piece. But even success was an illusion, as fragile and chimeric as the steam drifting off the backs of the horses pulling this very sleigh.

"You cold?" he asked. "You're shivering."

"Thin-blooded," she claimed. "All that southern California smoggy sunshine."

He put his arm around the back of her shoulders, drawing her against him for heat. "You get used to the cold up here after a while. I love the winters here."

"That figures. Because . . . skiing."

"Yeah. I still love being on the hill. But I also love a crackling fireplace, hot drinks, and the smell of Christmas trees year-round," he mused. "You, in green sweaters."

She blushed, then laughed. "I'm surprised you remember."

His smile broadened; his breath escaped him in a steamy cloud. "I remember a lot of things about us."

"Me too," she said, watching the dark shapes of trees slide by. "I remember long rides in your old VW bus, singing together to the terrible radio. I remember . . . the look on your face at the bottom of a spectacular run." She leaned her head back against his arm. "The night—kind of like this one—when you described barely escaping an avalanche that had chased you down a mountain."

"I remember that day. John Goehner and I were heliskiing up at Squaw Valley. We still talk about that run."

She rolled her eyes and tugged the blanket higher up around her. "That terrified me."

"You don't ski the way I did without a couple of close calls. It's just part of it."

"*Did*? What about now?"

"We were kids then. I still love to ski and board, but I don't take those kinds of risks anymore."

She stared at him with surprise.

"What?" he asked.

"I'm just shocked to hear you say that. Risk-taking was kind of your thing."

"Things change. There's a lot about me that might surprise you."

"Oh yeah? Like what?"

"Nah. Too easy. You'll have to figure that out."

"I see," she said with some amusement. "Well. I love a good mystery."

They rode for a while in silence, listening to the sounds of the woods around them. Above them, the winter sky was full of stars. Each hiding a mystery of its own. In LA, one couldn't see the stars for all the city lights. But here, the sky was awash in stories, connecting one star with the next by tales conjured by thousands of stargazers over the millennia. Seeing it looming so vastly above them made her feel small and insignificant. And all the problems she'd brought to the mountains with her seemed to fade away, here, leaning into Cole's warmth. It felt, for a little bit, as if it were just the two of them out here in the wilderness. Alone.

Giving herself a mental shake, she leaned back, away from his warmth. What in the world was wrong with her? What was she doing, waxing *poetic* about the night and the starry sky and the possibility of "them" when all he doing was trying to be nice?

The cell in her pocket buzzed, and she put a hand on her pocket to quiet it.

"You have to get that?" he asked.

She shook her head. "No. I definitely don't."

Soon enough, the ride pulled up at a clearing in the woods that was lit up like a Christmas tree, with lights strung everywhere and lanterns and paper-bag luminaries lining all the paths. The hotel had arranged the sleigh rides from the resort, but there was another entrance accessible by car and local visitors were already streaming in. It seemed to be an arboretum or park and she imagined how lovely it must be in the summer with its paved walking paths and now-frozen creeks that ran through it. The wide clearing at the center was dressed in twinkling white lights, which climbed the branches of the trees, and colored ones decorated sculptured bushes. The winter garden served as the hub for the spokes of trails that angled away into the luminary-dotted darkness. But she could see crowds moving slowly past strolling carolers down the trails.

She had all the feelings, looking at it, as Cole hopped down and extended a hand up to her, she murmured, "It's . . . it's so—"

"Sure is," he murmured, gaze pinned on her.

She hesitated for only a moment before taking his hand. "I was going to say it's so . . . *much*."

He just smiled. "I can see we're gonna have to work on your Christmas appreciation."

"I think we're in the right place for that," she said. "Do you see Quinn?"

They spotted him hopping around with the twins near Amy and her husband and their dog Alex. He dropped his hand from the small of her back as they drew closer to the others and Eden felt the lack acutely but kept space deliberately between them.

Amy introduced herself and her husband, Ken, to Cole. "So happy we get to meet your other half, Eden," she said, smiling up at Cole.

"Oh. Oh, no," Eden said quickly, exchanging an uncomfortable look with him. "We're not—"

"We're, uh, old friends," Cole explained for her.

"Ah," Amy replied, embarrassed.

"This isn't even a date," Eden explained with an uncomfortable laugh. "It's . . . it's . . . more like a reunion."

Amy and her husband nodded thoughtfully. Or curiously, it seemed.

"Then how come you changed all your clothes four times when you were getting ready?" Quinn asked.

She gave her son the side-eye. "*Quinn . . .*"

Amy bit back a smile and pulled Quinn into a quick hug.

"*What?*" Quinn asked Eden in all innocence. "You did."

Amused, Cole squinted into the darkness. Ken, a gregarious, pharma salesman type, clapped him on the shoulder. "So. How 'bout those Raiders?"

But Cole's eyes met hers for a moment, making it clear he was intrigued by this revelation.

"Oh-kay," Eden said brightly. "Well, now that we're here, which trail shall we take?"

"All roads lead to home," Cole answered. "That one looks nice." He pointed to the one with the fewest people on it.

"SO," COLE SAID as they fell behind Amy, Ken, and the boys. "Four times, huh?"

"Don't—" she warned with a horrified grin.

"I'm just sayin'. Four times. You must have wanted to impress me."

"No. It had nothing to do with that," she lied. "I just couldn't find anything to match my black jeans."

He nodded thoughtfully. "If it's any comfort, I went through a few shirts before I settled on this one."

"You *did*?"

He shook his head "no."

She socked him playfully in the arm.

Laughing, he dodged her. "Ow!"

"Okay, fine. I finally put on the green sweater because I remembered you loved that color and so I chose this. There. Happy?"

"Deliriously. You look great in it. If I may say so, it was worth giving your son something to tease you about."

"As if he needs an excuse. He's seven. And male. Enough said."

Chuckling, Cole crooked his arm and offered it to her. Without thinking too hard about it, she threaded her arm through his. They must have walked a mile and a half along the luminary-lit paths, sometimes lagging far behind the boys, who raced on ahead with the two dogs.

Halfway, they stopped at an oil drum fire station to warm their hands. The scent of the pinewood burning filled the clearing.

They stared into the orange embers glowing in the fire. She asked, "Do you live up here permanently now? Or are you still chasing the seasons?"

"Nope. I'm here now." He tucked his gloves in his pocket. "I bought a place down near the lake a few years back. I like it here, and I'm not in any hurry to leave."

"I remember that little cabin we used to drive by. You used to say we would live there someday. Did you buy it?"

He absolutely remembered it. In those days, that little cabin was as far as his ambitions carried him. It was a perfect little cabin. Room for the two of them, a stack of firewood. A future.

"No," he told her. "I didn't buy it. But mine's not far from there. I'm having a little Christmas gathering tomorrow night there if you want to come. Just a few people from the hotel.

"It's not until eight o'clock or so—Quinn's bedtime. I can even find you a babysitter for him if you want. I know of a good one who comes armed with her own Star Wars DVDs. Anyway, you could probably use one grown-up night on your own on your vacation. Right?"

"I don't know . . ."

"'Course, don't feel like you have to—"

"No," she said. "I mean, yes, that would be fun. Okay. Thanks."

He smiled. "Good. I'll give you my address, and put you

in contact with Karen."

They strolled a little farther and finally, Eden said, "That's nice you own your own little place now. I've been meaning to buy a place for years but the real estate market down there is crazy. Quinn and I love our little Venice rental house, and I keep hoping the landlord will decide to sell it to me. Then again, maybe we'll up and move to Paris one day. Or Florence."

"*Paris*? That's a little out of the box for you."

She shrugged. "Maybe the box has become a little too . . . *boxy* lately. I'd love to travel more. Take Quinn places. I've been working so hard for so long, and I'm not exactly sure of the end goal. More work? More money? Coming here, seeing Quinn be carefree and happy again, it kinda makes me wonder what I'm chasing."

"That's a change from the Eden I used to know."

"Oh, she's still here somewhere. But only slightly disappointed that her plan wasn't foolproof."

"Funny, how that works." Cole brushed back some twigs out of the way as she walked under them. Their eyes met under the canopy of branches.

"Yeah," she agreed.

He wanted to kiss her. Right here in the middle of the woods. Remember the taste of her. The soft press of her lips against his. He could have, with her face only inches from his, her eyes searching his with a welcome he hadn't expected. But another couple walked up behind them and passed them on the narrow trail with a friendly nod.

Eden began walking again, and the moment was lost.

They strolled in silence for a little while, not touching, before she said, "We shouldn't, you know."

"Shouldn't what?"

"You shouldn't kiss me."

"Why not?"

"I don't know. Self-preservation?"

"Yours or mine?" he asked.

"Both?"

"A kiss is just a kiss."

She flicked a look at him through her lashes and sang, "'A smile is just a smile . . .'"

"And you've still got the pipes." He'd always loved her singing voice. Even back when she could slay a song.

"Nice segue. Flattery will get you everywhere."

"Good to know. You still sing?"

She shrugged, looking embarrassed. "Sometimes. In the wee hours of office parties, after a couple glasses of wine."

"No more church choir?" She'd been a soloist for a few years at the church her parents attended. She joined mostly to sing, but he knew she'd enjoyed it too.

She frowned. "No. I couldn't find my way back there after Jo and Aaron died. The only one I really sing to now is Quinn."

Imagining that made him smile. When she spoke of Quinn, all the love she had for him was written so clearly on her face. That little boy had certainly changed her life. Changed her too. He could understand why.

He shoved his hands in his pockets, walking alongside her, his hand encountering that little Monopoly piece again.

"Speaking of Jo, look what I found in my pocket today. I have no idea where it came from, or how it got there." He produced the little silver top hat in the flat of his palm.

She stopped dead on the trail, the color leaving her face. She plucked it out of his hand and turned it over in her own. "That's weird. What do you mean you don't know where it came from?"

"It just . . . appeared in my pocket. Right after I tangled with a strange woman at the dog park. We ended up all wound up in dog leashes." He shook his head. "But that's probably just a coincidence."

"This one is old. See here? There's a few like it in Jo's collection, probably from 1945 or so, but this one's better. Even earlier. Maybe the thirties."

"I remember she collected these. We even played the game on her wedding weekend in a big tournament. In which I famously went down in flames on Park Avenue."

"And in which I famously won," she said, still turning the piece over in her hands.

"I shouldn't have been surprised you ended up in real estate. Whatever happened to her collection anyway?"

"Quinn has it now. In a place of honor in his room. He's got dozens of tokens, but he's still missing a few. Jo would always hunt them down. She was a nut for them. I don't think I've played the game since she died. Another thing I couldn't bring myself to do." The line between her brows furrowed deeper. "But why would a stranger put a Monopoly token in your pocket? I mean, for what?"

"You got me," he said. "She was a strange one. Friendly, but odd."

Eden raised a brow. "Sounds like someone I met the other day. Can I have this? For the collection?"

"Sure. I wouldn't want it to go anywhere else."

"Quinn will be thrilled. Speaking of him, do you see him up ahead?"

The boys had run on in the dark with the dogs, and even Amy and Ken had rounded a curve in the trail up ahead and disappeared. Eden and Cole picked up their pace and finally wound up at the main event, where there were refreshments, caterpillar tunnels of Christmas lights for kids to run through, and a Santa's village complete with throne. But it was crowded and they couldn't spot the boys.

There was an arts and crafts tent where parents crowded around their children three and four deep. "He's gotta be with Mack and the twins. Maybe," Cole suggested, "he's over there writing up a list for Santa."

She cut a look at him. "He's already given me his list. He's getting a bike for Christmas. Or a *picture* of a bike until we get home."

"A picture. How many Christmases you figure are left

before he leaves for college?" he said. "Nine? Maybe ten?"

"I know you're about to make a point here."

"Just that he's still little. Where's the harm in letting him believe for just a little bit longer?"

"Well, I'm afraid I can't put the toothpaste back in the tube. He asked and I told him the truth. Like I said, as romanticized as Santa, the tooth fairy and the Easter bunny are, lying to your kids is unproductive and perpetuating the myths of—"

"Maybe," Cole interrupted, gesturing in the distance with his chin, "he didn't altogether believe you."

She frowned and followed his gaze. A few dozen feet outside the small structure called Santa's Workshop, lit up by lanterns, the jolly old elf himself stood, hands on knees, bending toward her son who was whispering in his ear. Santa nodded and spoke for another few seconds with her son before handing him a lollipop and walking off into the dark behind the workshop.

Quinn spun toward her. Looking positively gleeful.

Eden blinked in surprise. She started toward the Santa lean-to, but Quinn spotted her first and ran in her direction. "Mom! Guess what? I wasn't going to talk to Santa, but Tyler said I should, or I won't get what I want. So, I did, and I told him that Mack wasn't mine, but I wanted a dog and he said yes!"

"H-he what?"

"He said I would get a dog for Christmas, and I didn't

even have to write him a letter."

"Oh, he did, did he? Maybe I'll just have a word with Santa then."

"Eden . . ." Cole warned, recognizing the determined look on her face.

"What? I'm just going to have a little chat." She scowled, and muttered under her breath, "With that misguided impersonator."

Cole took Quinn by the shoulders, distracting him in as Eden marched over to the workshop. "Hey," he said. "Did you tell him what kind of dog you wanted?"

"You don't get to pick your dog, Santa said. Dogs pick you."

Cole dug his fingers into Mack's thick fur. He had to agree with Santa on that one.

BY THE TIME Eden had worked her way past the crowds and the lines of children waiting to see Santa, she noted that he was not on his throne but working his way back over to it. Before he could take his seat, she managed to buttonhole his red velvet self and get a face-to-face with him. Really. The nerve of this stranger promising Quinn a dog.

"Hellooo there," Santa boomed over the din behind them in his fake Santa baritone. "I'm just about to sit down. If you want your little boy or girl to meet me, the line starts back—"

She snatched the man's arm and turned him away from the crowds. She kept her voice low but failed to conceal her irritation. "My little boy already met you, thank you very much. And, frankly, I'd like to know who you think you are?"

"*Ho-Ho-Ho*!" Santa bellowed with a wary look in his eye, forcing her to take a step back. "I'm Santa Claus, of course."

"Well, *Santa*, since when do you promise seven-year-old boys presents they're not going to get?"

He leaned in a fraction. "Lady," he whispered, "I never promise gifts. I only promise to remember them on Christmas. That's against union rules."

"Union rules. I see. So why does my son think you promised him the dog he's been begging for?"

"Dog? I never promised a dog. I think I'd remember that."

"Five minutes ago. My son stood right over there with you. I saw you hand him a lollipop!"

"Five minutes ago, I was on a break."

"Excuse me?"

He tugged her over further in the corner, signaling to his elf photographer to give him just another minute. "We're entitled to breaks, you know. I just got back from the trailer."

"So, you're saying it wasn't you? In the red suit and white beard. Leaning over my son."

He tilted a patient look at her past his wire rims and winked. "Nope."

"Then who was it?"

A five-year-old blonde girl with cute little braids snuck past the photographer and tugged on Santa's red velvet pants.

"Santa, Santa, I saw your reindeer in the woods!"

The imposter pulled the little girl in front of him like a shield against Eden's scowl. "*Ho-ho-ho*!" he boomed, raising a winged white brow at Eden. "Did you, now? Well now, that Blixen is a real troublemaker these days."

The child nodded, transfixed, until her mother came and tugged her back to the end of the line.

Not giving up, Eden leaned in. "If it wasn't you, who exactly is this 'other Santa' and where can I find him?"

"Billy's taking over my shift in an hour, but he hasn't arrived yet. But if he were here, he'd be in that trailer back there. But he's not."

Eden narrowed a look at him. "I *saw* a Santa. My son *spoke* to a Santa. And if it wasn't you—"

"Well—" Santa hitched up his red velvet pants with a little cowboy flourish. "It is Christmas, ma'am. And you know what they say."

"No, what do they say?"

"You're never too old to believe in the magic of Christmas." Santa pulled away from her and settled down on his golden throne. "Merry Christmas boys and girls! Who's got a

Christmas wish?"

As Santa's helper guided the first little boy, a toddler who immediately started crying, to Santa's lap, Cole, Quinn, and Mack appeared at the threshold of the workshop. Cole gestured at her to *step away* from the Santa.

Frustrated, Eden held up one finger, asking him to wait. *The magic of Christmas, my eye!* Someone was lying and it sure wasn't her. She walked back toward where Santa had pointed, toward the small trailer that apparently served as a break room for him and his partner in crime. As she lifted her hand to knock on the door, a small, white feather swirled toward her in the dark, landing on her shoulder. A few more swirled in the darkness, where she caught a glimpse of someone disappearing in the dark around a curve in the road—a retreating flash of a woman with dark hair in a forest-green wrap with a dark fringe. Or at least, she imagined she saw that. It was too dark to really be sure who she saw.

But she could have sworn it was—

"Eden," Cole called from somewhere behind her.

She whirled back toward him with confusion. He had his hand on Quinn's shoulder and both were staring at her in concern. Even Mack has his ears up at alert.

"You okay?" Cole asked.

"Yes!" she answered a little too quickly. "I'm fine. I . . . I just—" She glanced back at the darkness. *Strange.*

"You sure? You look a little pale. What are you looking

for back here?"

"No one. Never mind." She wrapped the loose ends of her scarf around her neck and forced a smile.

Quinn took her hand in his small one, something he rarely ever did anymore. "Don't worry, Mom. I'll talk to Mrs. Reedy." *Her landlord.* "She'll have to let us have a dog."

Unlikely. *Highly* unlikely. But she hugged Quinn to her. "Let's not worry about Mrs. Reedy now, Quinny. Or about a dog. Or about anything. Hey, I saw some donuts for sale over there. What do you say we get some? Powdered sugar, your favorite."

She met Cole's eyes over her son's head as Quinn agreed and bolted over to the donut tent. Anxious to follow him, Mack tugged at the leash Cole held. "Don't say it."

"Say what?"

"That I'm a Scrooge."

He peered into her eyes with a look that confused her and heartened her at once. "I wasn't going to."

"He'll forget about the dog," she assured him with as much confidence as she had that she hadn't just seen the mysterious Marguerite Ciel absconding into the woods. "And the promise from Santa."

"You're probably right," he said, and took her hand in his.

It had been so long since someone had comforted her in this simple way, she felt the shock of his touch travel up her arm and zing into her heart with a painful throb. She tried to remember if Wesley had ever done such a sweet thing, and she knew he hadn't. If he ever held her hand it was a precursor to something else and never a simple act of generosity. Deliberately pushing Wesley from her thoughts, she tightened her fingers around Cole's in gratitude.

They bought the sweet bites of donuts, said their goodbyes to Amy's family, and together took the sleigh back to the lodge. There was only a crescent moon lighting the dark sky, so along the way Cole pointed out a shooting star from the constellation Ursids behind the Little Dipper. This, he explained, was the time of year for the meteor shower, and he told Quinn he often came out on nights like this one to watch for them. He showed him how to find the Big Dipper off the handle of the Little Dipper. As the sleigh slid across the snowy trail, they all tipped their heads back to watch for more shooting stars. Of course, Quinn spotted the most. It was the best thing she had done in years.

For her son, it was a perfect night. She'd never seen him so blissfully content with the world as he was here, compared with the stressful life they lived down in LA, always on the go, go, go and never stopping for something so impractical as watching the night sky.

His ease with Cole was something to behold. Cole had a way with him, just as he still did with her. She'd missed him, but it was only beginning to hit her how much she'd missed him. Maybe she was imagining it or hoping that what had happened between them tonight was special. But as they walked back into the hotel, across the snowy yard, this felt more real than anything had felt for a long, long time.

As they walked through the double doors of the hotel's front entrance, Cole paused to speak to the bell captain.

"Mr. Hagar?" the tall, thirty-something man said with a nod and a broad smile as he held the door open for them.

"Thanks, Louden," Cole replied. "Hey, how's your mom doing?"

"So much better, thank you. She's been out of the hospital for a week now. Looks like she'll be celebrating Christmas with us, after all." He all but beamed as he said this.

"That's great to hear. Merry Christmas to you and your family."

"And to you, sir." Louden gave him a two-finger salute and tugged at the jacket of his uniform. "See you at the concert!"

"It's gonna be good," Cole told him as he ushered her and Quinn into the lobby.

"So, this concert," she said, as they walked through the tall atrium-sized lobby. "I've heard people talking about it. Sounds like it's going to be great. You going?"

"I am," he said. "I'm actually helping to organize it. It's the day after tomorrow and we're expecting quite a turnout for it. Let's hope we get one anyway."

She tilted a look at him. "Because . . . ?"

"Because," he said, "we need it to be good. The resort needs it to be good."

Eden swallowed hard. She knew exactly what he meant and pressing him on it felt wrong. But she was still doing a job here. "The resort seems busy enough," she said, though it was only in the last day that crowds had begun to fill up the hotel.

"It's been a little thin this year, with the snow and everything," he admitted. "But things are starting to pick up."

"I'm sure it will be good."

His smile made her feel awful.

"Our guests are heavily discounted for the concert. But I'm sure I can get you comped if you're going to be here for it."

As they got in the elevator and went up to her floor, Eden said, "Quinn and I would love to go. I heard Jason Tunney is going to perform."

"He's the big draw. We're excited he's agreed to come. As a favor."

"To whom?"

"Mostly to Granger Stuart, the longtime owner of this place. He's given many performers their starts here and has always been a supporter of musicians. Jason's career took off right here five or six years ago, and now he's big time in Nashville. Granger doesn't know it, but this whole concert is a tribute to him as he's about to retire."

This was news. News that might affect the whole future of this resort. Quinn pressed sleepily against her side as she studied Cole, trying to suss out what he wasn't telling her.

"You're pretty involved here, it seems like. More than just as an instructor."

"Being an instructor isn't my job here anymore," he admitted. "I do it once in a while because I still love it."

They walked off the elevator and arrived at her door. "So, it was just a weird coincidence that Quinn was in your class?"

"A nice one," he admitted, pulling another coin from behind her son's ear and handing it to him. "Where'd that come from?"

Loving it, Quinn giggled and pocketed the coin as Cole met her gaze with one so deep she couldn't read it.

"People call you Mr. Hagar. I've heard them. So exactly what is it you do here?"

He took her keycard and swiped it in her door lock. "Come tomorrow night. I'll tell you then," he said, opening it for her.

She tilted a confused look at him, the leaned down to Quinn. "Go on in and get ready for bed, honey. I'll be right in." Reluctantly, he shuffled through the door.

"Night, Quinn," Cole called after him.

Quinn turned around and hugged him a quick goodnight.

As the door shut behind him, Eden met Cole's steady gaze. "That never happens."

He smiled. "Must be the Santa thing."

"Please. Don't mention Santa," she deadpanned.

The laugh that escaped him reminded her of when they used to laugh together all the time. It changed his face so essentially; she wondered why he didn't do it more. Maybe it was her.

"Okay. Will you come tomorrow?"

She nodded. "You've got me curious."

"Good." He seemed to be having trouble containing his grin. He was standing so close, with his arm up bracing the wall over her head, and he had a small speck of powdered sugar on his cheek.

"Um, you've got a little . . . powdered sugar on your . . ." she reached up to brush it off, but he got there first and brushed off his cheek.

"Better?" he asked.

"Uh-huh."

His gaze slid over her face and lingered on her mouth. "I had fun tonight."

"So, did I. So did Quinn. It was great. Thank you for everything."

"Totally selfish on my part."

Was it? "Well, it was so nice catching up." She knew she should go in. Say goodnight and end this awkward pause between them. But she could no more pull herself away from him without touching him than she could make herself fall in love with Wesley. The thought of him made her lower her lashes, breaking eye contact with Cole.

He lifted her chin with one finger. "It's none of my business where you went just then, but I just want to say . . .if this is the universe's way of patching both of us up from the mess we made of our past, then I'm all for it."

A slow smile crossed her face. "Me too."

"You mean that?"

She squeezed her eyes shut, forcing back unexpected tears, and nodded.

"Hey." When she looked up again, he angled his head toward her, intending to kiss her, but searched her eyes first, hoping she wouldn't stop him. She leaned closer, unwilling to stop him. Wanting to kiss him. Wishing he would.

And then he did. Slowly. Gently. Thoroughly. His mouth covered hers in a kiss so familiar it made her insides drop with hunger. And as if all the years between them hadn't passed, his hands found the sides of her face and he pulled her toward him, deepening the kiss with his tongue. She welcomed him in and kissed him back. Reflexively, she flattened her palms against his strong chest, then slid them around his neck. Heat sang through her, making her insides dip and plunge. She felt branded by his mouth, his heat, and the dangerous currents between them. Everything in her yearned for more. But even as she did, sanity called her back from the brink of wanting more than she deserved. She pulled away from him and broke the kiss, breathless and feeling confused.

She thought of Wesley and the kisses they'd shared. His, she thought, were like a placid lake and Cole's the tumbling sea—alive with wildness underneath and the unknown.

Questioningly, he pressed his forehead against hers. "What are you afraid of Eden?"

"Everything," she whispered.

"Me?"

She touched the dark scruff on his jaw with the palm of her hand. "I just don't want to hurt you again."

"Life's too short to play it safe. I can take care of myself."

He was so right about life being short. Jo was proof. But playing with risk sounded so much easier than it was. "My life is not that simple, Cole."

"Neither is mine. That doesn't mean we can't meet somewhere in the middle."

She opened her mouth to respond but couldn't think of an answer to that. Her life was so much more complicated than she'd admitted to him. And she was quickly losing track of everything she thought she knew to be true.

"I wasn't looking for this," he said, brushing the hair away from her face. "I know you weren't either. I'm not even sure I know what 'this' is that's happening between us. But I want to find out. Look, I'm busy all day tomorrow with prep for the concert but come tomorrow night to my place. I want you to see my life. I want to know yours."

"Mine's in that room," she said, indicating her son. "He's my everything. Everything I never knew I wanted. Everything I never thought I could be."

He kissed her again, quickly this time. Just a quick, I-see-you kiss. A punctuation point on the night. "He's everything good that you are. And have always been."

Tears sprang uninvited to her eyes. No one had ever said such a thing to her, and she wasn't even sure she believed it. But she loved him for saying it. Even as she thought that, she realized how wrong it was that she didn't have someone in her life to treat her this way. "'Night, Cole."

Releasing her reluctantly, he pushed away and walked backward down the hall. "Tomorrow night. I'll text you the address."

She watched, half inside her room, until he disappeared into the elevator, then she closed the door behind her. What was she doing? What was she getting herself involved in here?

And more importantly, how was she ever going to tell him the truth about what she was doing here?

Chapter Seven

"JASON TUNNEY ISN'T coming, Cole."

Those five words from Lisa, the concierge, stopped Cole in his tracks. Dread sent cold fingers through his gut. "What do you mean he isn't coming? He's committed. For months now."

The worried look on Lisa's face said it all. "His manager, Edward Ainsley, called ten minutes ago. Said Jason is sick." She handed him the note she'd taken.

Cole stared at it in disbelief. "Sick? He'd better be freaking *dying*."

"His manager sent Jason's sincere apologies."

"Oh. Did he?" Running a hand through his hair, Cole paced in front of the concierge desk like a penned-up tiger. He'd bet his apologies were sincere. After all, if it wasn't for Granger, he wouldn't have a career now! "And Ainsley called you, instead of me?"

Lisa blushed, clearly wishing she wasn't the messenger. "I'm sorry, Cole. I told him he should speak to you, but—"

"Get him on the phone for me."

She winced. "He said to tell you he's not going to be

available as he's on vacation in the Bahamas, but he just said to pass on Jason's deepest apologies and best wishes."

"Then get Jason on the phone."

"I tried. He's not answering."

"The show is in—" he glanced at his watch "—forty-three hours and thirty-nine minutes. Half the people coming are coming specifically to see him. Where on God's green earth will I find a replacement for our headliner by then? I can tell you where. Nowhere. Where is he? Is he in the hospital?"

"Mr. Ainsley didn't say."

"Cole?"

Eden's voice came from behind him and he whirled around to find her and Quinn walking toward him. Just seeing her there lowered his blood pressure a notch. With her hair down and her cheeks reddened from being outside, she looked just as she had eight years ago when he'd fallen in love with her. "Eden."

"Is everything okay? You look upset."

"Hey, Q," he said, ruffling the boy's hair. "No," he told Eden. "Everything is not okay. But it's nothing for you to worry about."

"Please. Tell me," she insisted, exchanging looks with Lisa, who backed off immediately and buried her nose in the computer screen at her desk.

Cole glared off at the mountain outside the giant glass windows of the atrium. "My headliner for the concert just canceled on me."

"Jason Tunney?"

He sent Lisa a confirming look. "See? Yeah. Apparently, he's sick and can't make it."

Her face lost a little color. "Oh, no. I'm sorry, Cole. What'll you do?"

"What *can* I do at this point? The show's in two nights. No way I can get another artist to drop everything and bring his entire crew and band in that time. I really thought Jason was more dependable than this. But if you're sick, you're sick, right?"

"This concert," she said. "It's important to you. And to this place. Right?"

He couldn't read what was in her eyes just then as she asked that. Maybe just simple concern. But he could have sworn there was something else. Almost like she hoped he didn't say yes. But, of course, he did.

"This concert can make or break us," he said simply. "Yeah. It's important."

Eden drew Quinn in front of her, her hands on his shoulders. "And you're sure he's actually sick? You talked to him?"

"He's not answering his phone. But why would you say that? He's indebted to Granger for his whole career. Nothing short of dire illness would keep him from coming. Why else would he cancel?"

With a shrug, she allowed, "I don't know. It's been

known to happen. Things like this. It's a cutthroat world out there. I'm just saying—"

"As in . . . someone is intentionally sabotaging the concert?"

Her lashes cast shadows on her cheeks as she pulled Quinn toward her. "No, I'm sure that's not what happened."

"Well, if you have any helpful ideas, I'd be happy to hear them."

She nodded and smiled up at him. But even her smile felt off. Maybe it was the kiss last night that was on her mind right now. Maybe he'd scared her off. Or maybe once they talked, she'd clear things up. "I'm sorry. I'm so wrapped up in this. I didn't even ask how you were. You doing okay? You and Quinn?"

"Yeah. And listen, the concert has so many great people lined up, it will still be amazing."

Of that, he wasn't at all sure. "Seventy-five percent of our ticket sales have been because Jason was performing. This will not go over well."

He shook his head, feeling defeated. There were other good artists lined up for tomorrow night, but none as big as Jason. If this concert was a bust, so was the resort. This was his last-ditch hope that they could make up for the last few tough years. It was designed to draw people back to the resort, reintroduce the community to what had always made this place great, the thing that Granger had begun so many years ago. Disappointing the crowds that showed up would only bring bad press and bad feelings and damn sure wouldn't be converting them into returning guests. And it would be a sad, very bittersweet end for Granger too.

"Miss Kendall?" The young bellman Cole recognized as David Regan was holding an enormous, gorgeous bouquet of flowers as he walked up behind her.

Surprised, she turned. "Yes? I'm Eden Kendall."

"Room 3145, right?"

She eyed the flowers with a frown and nodded. "Yes?"

"I was just about to take these up to your room. They just came for you. Shall I take them upstairs for you?"

Eden glanced at Cole with a look that was at once surprised and horrified. "There must be a mistake. They can't be for me."

"Oh, yes. Says right here. There's a card." He shifted the lush bouquet of roses, hydrangeas and lilies in his arms.

A sinking feeling struck Cole. Who was sending her flowers like that? That didn't look like any casual *have-a-nice-vacation* bouquet. It looked more like a message from a serious lover.

Eden snatched the envelope off its spike. After reading it, she shoved it in her pocket. "You know what?" she told Regan. "There must be someone here in the hotel who needs these flowers. Can you please see that they get them?"

"But—" the bellman began.

She pulled some money from her pocket and shoved the tip in his hand. "Someone celebrating a wedding," she suggested, "or someone recovering from something. Maybe someone on the staff? I don't know. I'm sure you can find someone."

Regan nodded, passing a look with Cole. "Well, there is Julian Domingo. He's on our maintenance staff. His wife has been undergoing—"

"Perfect," she said. "Please give them to Mrs. Domingo. Thank you. So much."

"Yes, ma'am. I'm sure he'll . . . she'll appreciate that."

As the slightly befuddled Regan wandered away with the flowers, she met Cole's gaze. She shook her head above her son's as if to say she would explain later. But he knew no explanations were required. They'd both had full lives since they'd seen each other last. And though she hadn't mentioned seeing anyone else, he had no right to assume there wasn't someone else in her life.

No right, but the green specter rose in him just the same. He could draw all sorts of conclusions from what she'd just done, all but tossing the flowers in the trash bin, but until he heard the story behind them, speculation seemed less than useful. Maybe it was their history, or the fact that she'd been less than forthcoming with him about her life, but Cole instinctively felt his already slim chances with her take a Wall Street tumble.

"Secret admirer?" he asked as Regan disappeared into the backroom with the flowers.

"It's complicated." She tilted her head toward her son.

"They're from Wesley," Quinn told him matter-of-factly and with a little attitude. "He always sends her flowers."

Eden slid her hand down over her son's mouth in a playful, absolutely serious way. "Quinn."

Cole raised a questioning brow in her direction.

"They're nothing. The flowers. Can we talk about this later? Alone?"

"Hey, you don't owe me any explanations, Eden."

"I do. And I will explain. Just . . . not here."

"Listen, I've got to go. I've got to figure this Jason Tunney problem out, and I've got a million loose ends for the show and for the party tonight. You *are* coming tonight." It wasn't exactly a question.

"Am I?" she asked, with not a little uncertainty.

"Of course. Of course, you are. Karen's already agreed to stay with Quinn. Unless you don't want to?"

She was blushing now. "No, I-I do. I'll be there."

He smiled down at her. "Good. You two have plans today?"

"We're going inner tubing!" Quinn said. "Wanna come with us?"

"Wish I could, Q. But I've got to take care of some things."

Eden wrapped her hand around Quinn's shoulder and said to Cole. "We'll see you later?"

"Absolutely." But he watched them walk away with an uneasy feeling. As if he'd just walked into some quicksand

and he was sinking fast.

EDEN STOOD AT the top of the hill, watching her son flying down the hillside on his inner tube, alone this time, shrieking with both terror and joy. Personally, her backside still hurt from the last series of moguls they'd bounced over, and she had concluded that she was too old for this hill. At the bottom of the run, Quinn's inner tube flipped over, sending him sprawling into the snow.

Eden gasped, taking two steps in his direction, but he jumped to his feet, turned and waved up at her, then began the long trudge back up the hill.

She exhaled. Children were so resilient. So much more so than grown-ups, whose battle scars and sensible insecurities served to freeze them up rather than allowing them to enjoy all the lessons they'd learned in a lifetime full of mistakes. She wondered why that was. Why couldn't she have the wide-eyed optimism that her son still maintained as a natural part of his being?

Instead, she lived in her head, which frequently pushed her in the wrong direction out of pure fear. Optimism was the characteristic that had attracted her to Cole in the first place, if you didn't consider those eyes of his, or his beautiful body, or a thousand other things she still found powerfully attractive about him. But optimism—that dreamer sensibility that said everything would work out if you just had faith—was also the thing that had ended them. And yet, had brought her, full circle, back to him here. *Isn't that ironic?*

Which was why, she thought, pulling her phone from her inner pocket, she had no choice but to make this phone call. It was now or never. She would have preferred never, because this was a conversation she did not want to have. But she dialed Wesley up anyway. He answered on the first ring.

"There you are." He sounded happy to hear from her. In a moment, he wouldn't be.

"What have you done, Wesley?"

There was a pause on the other end, a chuckle. "Ah. You got the flowers."

"Yes. That's not what I'm talking about."

"Whoa. No thank you? No . . . 'I accept your apology for our convo yesterday, Wesley?'"

"I am not talking about the flowers, or the conversation that went south," she replied tightly. "You know exactly what I mean. Don't deny it."

"Well, I've been sitting here hoping you would call me and here you are. Must be this wishful thinking thing works."

"Two words, Wesley: Jason Tunney."

Another long, revealing pause stretched between them. "I hear he's a good singer. Too bad he's sick."

Eden's eyes narrowed. "I knew it. I knew that was you. It couldn't have been a coincidence that I mentioned the concert to you and the next day the headliner drops out!"

"'Course it was me," he admitted. "But Eden, it should've been you."

"*Me*?"

"This is your job," he told her. "To make this deal happen. To find the vulnerabilities. So at least I can tell the old man you found a good one for me. He'll be happy with you. He might even promote you."

Promote her? Based on a dirty, underhanded trick? To Wesley, this was all just a game, like *Jenga*! where pulling out a vulnerable block held the key to the resort's inevitable downfall. Nicole had warned her. And she'd walked right into his plan. She felt foolish and naïve for not realizing what was happening earlier. But this was the first time undoing an entire business had become personal. And her up close view of it had changed everything.

She had to fix this. "It was the wrong thing to do, Wesley. Undo it. Undo it now. I swear, if you don't, I'll—"

"If I don't—you'll what?" he asked sounding offended. Surprised and offended. "Eden, what's this about? You seem to be taking this awfully personally."

She paced on the snowy hill, watching her son trudge toward her. He'd soon be close enough to hear. "My life is personal, Wesley. What I do to people is personal. There are real people here. Working people with jobs that support their families. What we do is strip them of all that and sometimes those jobs never come back."

"Some will get rehired. Maybe lots of them. But we've been doing this for years. What's with the sudden pang of conscience?"

"It's one thing when a company is up against the wall with no choice but to sell. But this. This is different. So, yes, I take it personally when we don't play fair. When a company could well survive if not for our interference. When we cheat."

"There is no cheating in business, Eden. There's only the winners and the losers. I did what had to be done. Sometimes a business that's tipping just needs a little shove. Nothing wrong with that. It's done all the time."

"Yes. I'm sure you're right. It's just not okay with me."

"Just come back home, Eden. Everything will be all right if you just come back to LA where you belong."

She inhaled deeply, trying to calm herself down. "Tell me. Do you like magic, Wesley?"

"What?"

"How about dogs? Do you like dogs? Or kids?"

"Now you're just talking crazy."

"Am I?" she asked. "Maybe suddenly, I'm making sense. Maybe somewhere back there I lost track of what I wanted and who I was. Maybe Quinn showed me that."

She could almost hear him paying attention suddenly. "Are you seeing somebody else, Eden. Is that it?"

"I can't marry you, Wesley."

"Wait a minute—"

"Because I'm not in love with you." There, she'd said it. "You should find someone who loves you completely. Someone who shares your point of view. Who wants what you want."

"You want what I want. I know you. You're just as ambitious as I am."

"I thought I was. I was wrong. And I am going to try to undo what you've done here. And if I'm fired, then so be it. Maybe that's the best thing."

A rosy-cheeked Quinn crawled up the last of the slope, dragging his inner tube with a huge smile on his face. "Did you see me, Mom? I got all the way down, and I got bumped off!"

"Eden?" Wesley warned through the phone. "Eden, you listen to me—"

She smiled down at Quinn. "I saw! You were amazing!"

"This time you come down with me!" Quinn tugged on her hand and pulled her toward the edge.

"Gotta go," she told Wesley. "Goodbye."

"Eden!" she heard him shout just before she hung up.

"Ready?" she asked Quinn. And piled atop one another, they sailed down the slope, laughing and shrieking together, shouting, "*Whee-ee-e*!"

THAT NIGHT, EDEN took an Uber to the address Cole had

texted her. Sitting in the backseat of the driver's car—a woman named Nanda—Eden watched the cabins and glass-windowed houses glide by. They were surrounded by giant fir trees and melting drifts of snow, remnants from the last storm. Everywhere, Christmas lights decorated windows, lampposts, and shops. There were shoppers out in the chilly evening, walking two by two, or arm in arm. Couples, friends, families. The pace here was so different from where she lived, where everything was fast. Fast traffic, overscheduled days that ended with fast food eaten quickly before homework, a fast story before bed, and the day was gone.

Here, it felt like people actually breathed. Took in that mountain air, inhaled the spruce scent that stores in LA sold in bottles and applied to warm light bulbs or fake trees for Christmas. Why, she wondered, hadn't she noticed this the last time she was here? Was she too young for such a pace to appeal to her or was she just old enough now to appreciate the difference?

She had to come clean to him. Tell him the truth about why she'd come here.

Don't think about the consequences. That was Nicole's advice. And it was sound, Eden supposed, if you didn't mind dealing with the aftermath of your inadvertent lies and omissions. But she did mind. She'd become very clear on that.

She tilted her head back and stared up at the stars through the back window. This was all Jo's fault. For dying and leaving her to navigate this road alone. And if not for Quinn, Eden probably would never have even run into Cole here, playing Santa Claus and teaching her son that magic was real. Somehow, Jo had managed to put Eden on a collision course with the man who'd hijacked a piece of her heart so many years ago.

As much as Jo loved her—and she had, fiercely—she'd never approved of Eden's decision eight years ago to walk away from him. "Short-sighted," was what she'd called her breakup with Cole, even though Eden had not asked for her advice.

"You'll get it one day," Jo had told her then, on the eve of the birth of what would be her first and only child, "when you realize that Mr. Perfect isn't out there, but Mr. Right just might be the one you walked away from."

It had only taken eight years for her to see the absolute truth in those words, though her admonition had an eerie way of echoing in her dreams more frequently than she cared to admit. And tonight she was on the brink of losing it all again if she couldn't make things right.

I will. I will make things right.

She'd considered telling him tonight, but spoiling his party was the last thing she wanted. Morning was soon enough. After she'd fixed this mess that she'd gotten him into, she'd tell him.

Nanda, a beautiful woman with long dark hair and chocolate colored eyes, tapped her Waze app and turned off the main road toward the lake. "Oh, this is very nice down here," she said, glancing in the rearview mirror.

If rustic cabins were your thing, she thought, as they drove past a few dozen summer places with funny signs hanging out front, like "What Happens at the Lake is Laughed About All Year Long," and "No Wi-Fi Here. Talk to Each Other!" and an arrow pointing to a quaint little brown cabin saying, "You Are Here." That one reminded her of the little house they'd wanted to buy one day. The cabin with probably three rooms altogether. Possibly indoor plumbing.

Once upon a time, she'd imagined such a house was everything. And maybe it still was, if it were here. After all, there was no one to compete with here at the lake. No one telling her what or who she needed to be.

"Going to a party?" Nanda asked. "I only ask because you look all dressed up and pretty."

"Oh, thank you," Eden said, smoothing a hand across the Swiss-dot fabric of the cranberry colored Draper James dress she'd worn. It was the only dress she'd brought with her to the mountains, just in case a meeting popped up. She hoped it was appropriate for Cole's intimate little gathering. "Yes. A small party. A few people, I think."

"Very nice," the woman said. "Many of these houses are second or third homes to the people who live here. Your friend must be a big deal. Up this way, everyone is."

"No, no," she said. "He's a skier. I think he has some part-time gig at the Four Winds Resort."

"Part time . . . hmm," the woman said, unwilling to argue, but flicking a disbelieving look at her in the rearview anyway. "Getting close now. Let's see . . ." She slowed to watch the house numbers as the homes got bigger and bigger. Elaborate, lakefront properties with gorgeous homes built into the side of the hill. Many were alight with Christmas trees in their windows and strung with lights around the house. Finally, she slowed at a line of cars, waiting for valet parking attendants to relieve them of their vehicles. "I think that's it," the driver said.

"What's it?"

The woman pointed to an enormous house, a contemporary log cabin design with beautiful picture windows overlooking the lake and at least three floors. The place was lit up like a Christmas tree, and even from here she could see the house was already filled with people—a lot of people—inside, heading up the walkway, standing on one of the three balconies that overlooked the lake.

"That can't be right," Eden said. "Are you sure that's the correct address?"

The Waze app announced, "You have arrived at your destination."

"Uh . . . yes," Nanda shut off the app. "This is it."

Stunned, Eden leaned back against the seat, staring at his house. How in the world? And *what the heck?*

The driver got out and opened Eden's door. "Have a nice evening, Ms. Kendall."

"Oh! Yes." She exited the car as gracefully as she could. "Thanks so much for the ride."

"Merry Christmas!"

"And to you too," Eden replied.

Feeling as if she'd dropped into an alternate universe, she climbed the long stone stairway up to his house. The front porch was the kind she'd always dreamed of, with a portico and white rockers perched under a log-raftered roof. Several couples approached the door ahead of her, and she was grateful for the delay. If this was Cole's house, everything she thought she knew about him was wrong. Everything she'd imagined she would know about him was wrong. And this was no intimate gathering. There were people from the hotel here. People who worked there that she recognized. It looked more like . . . a company party.

Inside, a sweet, dark-haired woman welcomed her, took her coat, and checked it into a make-shift coat room. Eden stared at the high ceilings, the beautiful light fixtures, and the farmhouse/cabin design of the house. Everywhere was comfortable seating, an eclectic mixture of antiques and modern furniture, every piece of which was occupied by a partygoer. There seemed to be a wide mix of people here, in both age and economic level, but one thing was clear from the first moment she walked in—they all seemed happy to be there and they all seemed to know each other. Like a family.

As she moved through the crowd, she searched for Cole but couldn't spot him. The man she'd seen playing the piano at the resort was sitting at the baby grand in the corner of the living room, playing "Little Drummer Boy." Three partygoers were standing beside him, turning his sheet music and singing the lyrics. And they were good. And not just karaoke good. Very good.

Two fully decorated Christmas trees graced the room, both covered in twinkling white lights and retro ornaments. Feeling conspicuously alone, she walked over to one of the trees to inspect it. Or rather to give herself the appearance of being occupied. But the ornaments were beautiful and looked like they'd been collected from places all over the world. There were winged blown glass birds, handcrafted miniature Swiss chalets, a pair of crossed skis from Austria, a blown glass bottle of wine from France. These represented his travels all over the world and answered a few of the questions she had about what he'd been doing since they'd split up. But—she glanced around the beautiful home he called his—not all her questions.

A mostly empty tray full of drinks swung by her and she gratefully snagged a glass of bubbly. "Thank you," she started to say to the uniformed server, but the woman had already turned away, heading back to the kitchen. Eden stared after her, thinking her retreating form looked familiar but she was surely mistaken.

"You look gorgeous," came a deep voice from behind her. Eden whirled to find Cole smiling at her. "Hi."

Predictably, her heart caught in her throat at the sight of

him. Gorgeous. Yes. He was.

"Hi, yourself." Her gaze drifted momentarily down the elegant but understated wool black sports coat he wore over an open white shirt. His holey, casual jeans had given way to intact, dark indigo ones that fitted him the way jeans should fit a man's body.

"Did you just get here?"

She swallowed thickly and lifted her glass of champagne. "Uh-huh. And it's . . . well, it's quite the place you have here. And it's really yours?"

"All mine," he admitted with a grin.

She blinked at him. "Working for the resort?"

A pair of partiers—a man and a woman—wrapped their arms around Cole's shoulders from behind in a hug. "You know how to throw a party, Mr. Hagan. Is the rink open? We were thinking of skating."

Eden's eyebrows went up. "The *rink*?"

Cole clapped the man on his shoulder. "If you want skates, there should be plenty down there. Find a pair and have at it."

As the pair disappeared into the partiers, Cole said, "It's just a thing I do in the winter here when it's cold enough."

"And the skates?" she asked incredulously. "You just keep dozens of pairs on hand?"

"Rented from a local rink. A real rink. We can go skating later if you want."

She glanced down at her flimsy, not very warm dress. "I

don't know . . ."

"Don't worry. I've got you. C'mon. I'll show you around." He took her hand, as if that were the most natural thing in the world, and tugged her through the partygoers, introducing her along the way. Many of them she'd seen in the hotel behind the front desk or on the ski hill. She even spotted a few of the wait staff from the restaurant singing along to the piano player's carols.

"An intimate little party, you said," Eden commented as they moved from the living room to a gorgeous kitchen with marble countertops and elegantly rustic cabinets. The catering staff was bustling through the room with trays and delicious-smelling hors d'oeuvres. Her stomach grumbled. "Just a few people, you said."

He grinned. "It's pretty intimate. They're all friends."

"Employees?"

"That too." Cole plucked a pair of yummy looking honey-drizzled baked figs stuffed with goat cheese off a server's tray and handed her one. "Try this. It's amazing."

The taste of it exploded in her mouth. "Mm-mm. Ohh . . . Where in the world did you get fresh figs this time of year?"

He grinned and pulled a coin from behind her ear, handing it to her. "Like that."

"Magic, huh? Somehow I think imports were involved."

"Possibly. You're just supposed to eat and enjoy."

"Oh, I am." She polished off the last of it, moaning with

pleasure.

There were two living rooms and a library filled with books—many first editions—and art everywhere from local sculptors and painters. A wide stairway led to the second floor but most of the guests were on the main level and the walk-out basement downstairs that led out to the expanse of flat land that held the small but perfect hand-sprayed ice rink. It was surrounded by small, Christmas tree-sized pines and lit by strings of twinkling electrical lights hung around the perimeter. A handful of couples were already out there skating.

Standing on the balcony, suddenly alone when two other couples wandered inside, she turned to him with a questioning look. The night air was cold, but for some reason, she felt warm standing beside him.

"What?" he asked, all innocence.

"You know what. Are you gonna tell me? Or are you going to make me guess how all this happened?" She gestured at his beautiful home. "From skiing?"

A shrug lifted his shoulders. "Skiing was just the road I took. Actually, snowboarding."

"Now you absolutely must explain." She could hardly tamp down the feeling of dread that had been creeping up her throat from the minute she'd seen this place. Found that he was not at all who she thought he was or ever would be.

"I spent the first few years after 'us' skiing, mixing it up with snowboarding. I liked it and spent months perfecting my carving stance, backslides, 360s. But I wasn't a kid anymore, and putting up with the chatter of the board was killing my knees and my feet. So, I set to work designing a dampening binding that would my cushion me better. I made a mockup and tested it for a while, modified it, then showed it to a friend of mine, a professional boarder with a hookup sponsorship to a big company that manufactures bindings. Long story short, they bought my design and cut me a generous piece. A very generous piece."

She remembered to close her mouth only when he'd finished. "You invented a binding?"

"I . . . restructured a binding. To make it more comfortable."

"And then what?"

Indicating the crowd inside his home, he said, "And then, I bought into the resort. The Four Winds was a place I already loved, and Granger Stuart was the godfather of the resorts up here. The old man on the mountain. But he was struggling a little to keep up with the newer, bigger corporate resorts that came in with lots of money. He needed an influx of cash and I had it. So, I became a partner."

Chapter Eight

EDEN FELT THE blood leave her face and felt a wave of sudden nausea. "You're . . . a *partner?* At the Four Winds?"

"Yeah. It was kind of a dream of mine anyway. And that binding made it all possible."

A dream. He'd been full of dreams once and none of them had seemed reachable. At least to her, a girl from a family of dreamers whose dreams had come to nothing but constant struggle. But she had underestimated him. Underestimated the power of his dreams, perhaps and, instead, put her faith in her own plans—her pragmatic, by-the-book plans that didn't allow for the elastic future he saw so long ago. No, she had sandwiched herself into someone else's dreams—Wesley and his father's—which had landed her here, shadowboxing the dreams of the only man she'd ever really loved.

She wouldn't cry now, not in front of him. She wouldn't. "That's so amazing, Cole. I'm so happy for you," she said haltingly, "And when Granger Stuart retires, it's all yours?"

With a frown, he touched the moisture at the corner of her eye. "Hey. What's this?"

She brushed her eye. "It's the cold air. It's nothing. I'm happy for you. That's all."

Pulling her up against him, he hugged her for a long moment until she could hear the beat of his heart against her ear, its steady rhythm pounding at the emotion in her throat.

"Why didn't you tell me before?" she asked. "Last night, when we were out?"

"I don't know," he murmured against her hair. "I think I didn't want that interfering with us yet. I wanted to strip all that away until we had a chance to really see each other again."

"Understandable," she conceded, pulling away from him and leaning her elbows on the railing. "Considering why I left in the first place. Even then, I never really deserved you."

He started to disagree, but she stopped him. "No. I've seen how these people love you, the life you've made for yourself here. What you've done. Turns out you were right about all of it. Having dreams, living the life you wanted to live. And I was wrong to sacrifice all that. I mean, I really have done what I set out to do, all those lists. Checked off all the things I wanted: to be secure, stable, financially safe, all that. But I . . . well, I never sing. Or paint. Or trust myself. I was dating a man I knew I could never love. And who I might have actually settled for if not for Quinn."

"The flowers?"

She nodded. "It's over. I should have told you about him, but—"

"You don't owe me any explanations," he said. "We both have lives. We're grown-ups."

"Maybe, but I wanted you to know. Quinn didn't like him. I'm seeing that more clearly now. He's been a different boy since we came here. Happy."

"He had some big losses when he was young. He's a great kid. That's all you."

"I wish I could take credit. Mostly I question whether Jo made the right choice in me."

From somewhere down on the ice rink, came the sound of jingling bells and laughter. A couple darted in the circle of light on the ice, chasing one another.

"Quinn's lucky to have you," Cole disagreed. "And Jo couldn't have made a better choice."

"Why are you being so nice to me?"

"I'm not being nice. It's just the truth. Whether or not you believe me. I've seen you with him and I've seen him without you. Kids are true reflections of the people who raise them . . . in my experience."

She shivered and hugged her arms around her. "I wish Jo and Aaron were still here for him. I wish Jo was still here for me."

Staring out at the starry sky, he murmured, "You never know . . ."

She followed his gaze. "Right. Like Santa and the unicorns?"

"Yeah," he said. "Like them."

Jo. Watching over her. "It would be nice to think so."

Down below, the couple stopped to kiss on the ice and when they'd finished, the girl shook her little bell bracelet, beckoning the guy to follow her off the ice. They could hear them talking but couldn't make out their words. Just as well. Eden was lost in her own thoughts. Particularly about Cole and the fact that his revelation spelled very bad news for her. "So, this resort," she began, "The Four Winds. It'll be all yours then when your partner retires in a little while?"

"Pretty much. He'll have his share, of course, and if he wants to, he'll advise me on operations. It's more than I imagined walking into this, but I never wanted to be a silent partner. I knew skiing and boarding wouldn't last forever. At least, not in the way I wanted to do it. And this place cried out for reinvention. To bring it up to twenty-first-century standards, environmentally and technologically. And we've done that. We just have to get the community to catch up to our innovation and come back. That's why this concert is so important. If it's successful, we'll stave off the wolves for a little bit longer, while we shore up the dikes."

The wolves. He was talking about her, without even realizing it. *Tell him. Tell him right now who you are. Tell him!*

"Cole," she began, "there's something—"

"Well, hello you two," came a female voice from behind them. "I've been looking everywhere for you, Cole."

Eden turned to find Cole's friend, Cat, smiling from the doorway in her slinky red party dress with a slit up her thigh and an unapologetic smile on her face. She looked completely different out of her Mrs. Claus outfit. Completely stunning. And she couldn't be more than twenty-five. She had a wildness to her with her pixie-short blonde hair that spiked carelessly around her face, tattoos that graced the side of her neck, her ankle—and other places, Eden could only imagine—and a wicked sparkle in her ice-blue eyes that was meant for Cole alone.

"Am I interrupting again?" She lifted her glass of wine with a smile.

Cole frowned slightly, but said, "Nope. We're just catching up out here."

They were doing more than that, but Eden wasn't about to argue.

"Well, I hate to break up this sweet reunion, but someone said the valet parking guy is looking for you."

"Really?" He straightened. "What for?"

"Some crisis with the parking and the neighbors?" she said, wandering out onto the patio, rubbing her arms to ward off the chill. "I guess he was kind of adamant about speaking with you."

Cole sighed. "I'd better go see what that's about. I'll be right back."

"Go." Eden smiled and waved him off and he disappeared inside. She was about to follow him, but Cat wandered over to the rail, seeming to want to talk.

"So, you're old friends, huh? You and Cole?"

"You might say that." Eden hid behind her wine glass while taking a sip.

"And your son—was it Quinn?—he's a little charmer. You and your husband must be very proud."

Eden just smiled at her. She knew where this was going.

"You *are* married I assume?" Cat blinked, waiting for a reply. "Oh. Sorry. I shouldn't assume, I guess."

"Assumptions can get you into trouble," Eden offered. "In my experience."

Cat sipped the last of her wine and set the glass down on the rail. "You're so right. Take Cole, for instance. Some people might assume he's an easy touch because he's so generous and kind to everyone. He's fiercely loyal to the people he cares about. But I know, for a fact, that he doesn't trust easily and believe me, you don't want to get on his wrong side by betraying that trust. I've seen that happen."

Eden felt her cheeks heat. "I'm sure you're trying to make a point here, Cat, but I wish you'd get to it because I'm freezing out here."

Cat turned to her directly. "Just that you're here on vacation while the rest of us live here, day in, day out, making the success of the Four Winds a reality. Some of us—me included—have Cole's best interests at heart."

"And I don't?"

"Do you?" she challenged.

"Sorry, but I honestly don't think our relationship is any of your business."

"Maybe. Then again, maybe more than you think. See, he's probably forgotten that he mentioned your name once to me. I think you're the reason he has so much trouble trusting women," Cat said frankly. "Yeah, he told me about you. How it ended between you two. So, if you're just going to drop in, steal his heart again, and leave, I'm asking you . . . don't. He doesn't deserve that. And besides that, *I* want him."

Just as Eden opened her mouth to reply, the door swung open again and one of the female wait staff backed through the door with half a tray full of wine glasses. Not just any waiter, she realized as the woman turned toward them. It was Marguerite Ciel!

"More wine ladies?" she asked in her polite Cajun drawl.

Before Eden could pull herself together enough to reply, Cat had grabbed a glass off the tray with an "I will," and took a quick chug, but immediately slapped her hand to her mouth, gagged, and pulled out—

"Eww! What the—?" Cat exclaimed, spitting out what wine was left in her mouth and examining the spindly thing between her fingers. "Oh my God. Is that . . . a . . . a *feather?*" She shook her fingers to rid herself of the wretched thing, accidentally whacking the wine tray so that the remainder of the glasses tipped and spilled down the front of her beautiful red dress.

"Oh! Look what you've done. You idiot!"

"Oh, I'm so terribly sorry," Marguerite told her in a most sincere voice, handing Cat some napkins. "Please forgive my clumsiness." She winked at Eden.

Eden did a double take, not sure she'd seen what she thought she had.

Overwrought now, Cat swiped at her soaked dress with the damp napkins and shook off her hands. "Just look at me. You've ruined my dress and the whole party for me! I am going to have a serious word with catering about you. You will be fired before the night is over!"

"Well, bless your heart, darlin'," Marguerite cooed, standing the empty wine glasses back up on her tray as Cat took her leave, slamming through the inside door and disappearing into the house.

Outside, Marguerite and Eden stared at one another, then started giggling.

"Well . . . nobody's perfect," the older woman conceded, wiping the wine off her starched uniform.

"Thank you. You saved me," Eden told her. "But what are you doing here? I thought you were a guest at the hotel. Do you work there?"

"No, no," she said, setting her tray down on the railing. "I pick up odd jobs here and there. This one just came up. I like to stay busy."

"I'm afraid Cat will put an end to this job for you."

Marguerite inhaled the sweet night air deeply. "Oh,

that's alright. Somethin' else will come along."

"Wait. Was that you the other night at the luminaria walk? I thought I saw you there."

"Sorry?"

"Were you filling in for Santa?"

That made her laugh with a belly laugh that sounded vaguely like *ho-ho-ho*. "Filling in for—? Whoever heard of a female Santa?" she asked. "And what use would they have for a *vielle* like me?"

"Hmm," Eden said, not sure if she believed her. "Because this particular Santa promised my son a dog for Christmas. A dog he can't have."

"Promised him?" she hedged. "That definitely breaks the rules. But as I said, boys and dogs, they find each other when they're meant to. Kinda like people, if you catch my meanin'. Findin' each other as their true course, when all along they had another direction entirely in mind."

Eden agreed, canting a look at her. "If I didn't know better, Marguerite, I'd say you were spying on me."

"Spying? *Moi?* Heavens, no." But intrigued, she added, "Do I *look* like a spy to you?"

"You look like . . ." an amused Eden speculated, "someone I should get to know better."

Marguerite chuckled. "Well, I'm only here temporarily. I'll move on soon. When my job here is finished."

"Which may happen sooner rather than later, if Cat has anything to say about it."

The older woman sighed. "Don't you be worryin' none about her, now. I'll be just fine. And so will you. If you listen to your heart and not your head." At Eden's suspicious look, she added, "It's plain as the nose on your face, *cher*. You are in a Christmas quandary."

"Exactly!" she confessed, leaning back over the railing. "My head is confused by what my heart is doing right now."

She patted Eden's arm with her plump hand. "My mama always used to say when I felt lost, 'watch for the signs. They're left like markers to guide you along the way. If you pay attention. Because the people you love never truly leave you.'"

Eden frowned, having just that moment thought about Jo. Marguerite winked at her again as the door opened onto the balcony and Cole reappeared. The woman scooped up her tray from the railing and bundled toward the door with her head down.

"Wait—" Eden called.

"Got to go now!" she called over her shoulder as Cole made way for her to sneak past him. And she disappeared inside.

"What was that about?" he asked, staring after the woman.

"I don't really know," she answered, meeting those kryptonite eyes of his that were watching her with concern. "Is everything okay with the valet?"

"There was apparently no problem with the valet," he

said, sounding irritated. "I don't know who Cat was talking to, but I'll get to the bottom of it later. You must be freezing. Let's go inside."

He wrapped a strong arm around her shoulders and guided her back inside where the warmth of the house seeped into her like a balm. His touch, his steady assurance, calmed her down. In her years working for Wildwood, she'd known a dozen women like Cat, and had learned how to deal with them, but what she'd said about not breaking Cole's heart again was a little too close to home. While Marguerite's appearance was another matter altogether. And she couldn't stop thinking about Marguerite and what she'd said. And how odd it had been to see her again. Here.

She half expected to hear Cat yelling at the catering staff about Marguerite as they walked into the kitchen, but everything seemed to be humming along without a ripple. Nor did Marguerite seem to be anywhere. But she felt compelled to put in a word for her.

The head caterer was buzzing around a tray full of tomato, basil, and goat cheese crostini, drizzling it with thick balsamic.

"I just wanted to say," Eden began, "It wasn't her fault."

The woman looked up. "Whose fault?"

"Marguerite's. She was really just being helpful, and the feather could have happened to anyone." That might have been a stretch, but it certainly hadn't been intentional.

The caterer straightened. "Are you talking about what

Cat was going on about?"

"Yes. I just wanted to tell the other side of the story."

Cole twisted a look at Eden, confused.

"I told Cat and I'm telling you," the caterer said, "that I don't have anyone named Marguerite on staff tonight. No one even fitting her description."

"What? But she was serving wine and wearing—"

"Nevertheless," the caterer interrupted, pulling her focus back to her crostini. "I can't fire someone I didn't even hire. Case closed."

"That's odd."

"What's this about?" Cole asked her.

"Nothing for you to worry about, Mr. Hagan," the woman said. "It's all under control."

"Good. That's what I want to hear," he replied with a nod, but to Eden as they left the kitchen, he asked, "Did something happen with you and Cat?"

"Nothing I can't handle," she said, still bothered by the caterer's words.

He smiled at her and took her hand. "You don't mind if I do this, do you?"

She shook her head. "I like it."

They mingled with the other guests and ate until they couldn't anymore. People were kind to her and welcomed her in, pulling her into their conversations and circles. Cole stayed with her, making her feel comfortable around his friends. And they all seemed like friends here, despite his being their boss.

Their boss.

Eden couldn't wrap her brain around how complicated his ownership of the resort made everything. She couldn't tell him the truth tonight and ruin his party. She'd have to tell him tomorrow, when this evening was behind him. When she'd fixed what needed to be fixed with the damage Wesley had done. She'd made a series of phone calls today after inner tubing with Quinn and it remained to be seen if her efforts would work. Then, at least, she might have a shot at making Cole understand her part in all of this. For tonight, the best she could do was to enjoy being with him and show him how she felt. This whirlwind week of emotions had gone from her avoiding him, to trying to convince him she wasn't that same girl who'd left him so long ago. The real question was—who was she now? Actions spoke louder than words.

I know, for a fact, that he doesn't trust easily and believe me, you don't want to get on his wrong side by betraying that trust.

Cat's warning rippled through her as the piano music started up again. Of course, she was right. She'd hardly have a leg to stand on tomorrow. He would have every right to think the worst of her for not telling him the truth. But it was too late to change that now. Now the best she could do would be to protect him. Minimize the damage. She just wasn't sure how.

A few of the guests at the party pulled out guitars they'd

brought along, apparently knowing this sing-along was coming, and another began playing his harmonica. The crowd began to sing along with pianist's version of "Have Yourself A Merry Little Christmas."

Sitting beside her, Cole began to sing along with the rest of them, his baritone voice sounding so familiar to her as she remembered many sing-alongs around the campfires in the summer at the beach and up here when they were together. He nudged her with a smile, encouraging her to sing along too. So she did.

And the roomful of people—Cole's people—all sang that old Christmas favorite together, with the white lights twinkling and the fire in the huge fireplace crackling. For the first time in a long time, just for a moment, Eden felt like part of a real community, while wishing her own troubles out of sight.

She felt him watching her as she sang. When she looked, he was smiling at her.

"See?" he mouthed. "You're singing again."

Chapter Nine

BEFORE THE NIGHT was over, after most of the guests had left, they skated on his ice rink. Cole let her borrow his heavy jacket, gloves, and hat, and together did laps around the icy circle in his yard with him holding her arm so she didn't fall. He knew the ice wasn't perfect. But that was the beauty of it. There were thin spots at the edges and bumps here and there. Neither of them minded at all.

The night couldn't have gone better and everyone had seemed to have fun. Great food. Great company. And Eden.

She seemed to have enjoyed herself tonight, though there were moments when she looked far away. He couldn't put his finger on what was troubling her, but he guessed that Cat had said something that bothered her.

Never in his fantasies of meeting up with her someday did he dream up a scenario in which they might find their way to each other again. But he was starting to see that possibility as something real. Something he wanted. He'd spent most of his life since she'd left him on the outside looking in at other people finding love, making a life together. For a long time, he'd decided it just wasn't for him. And like a self-fulfilling prophesy, he'd distanced himself from even the possibility and focused on work. Throwing himself wholeheartedly into work had saved him in a way, but at the same time, kept him at arm's length from any of the women he'd dated. But none of them was Eden. And therein lay the rub.

"Thanks for inviting me tonight," she said, as they took their last spins around the rink.

"It wasn't at all what I expected."

"Better or worse?" he asked.

"Better. To be sure, better."

He thought she'd enjoyed every minute of tonight apart from Cat. But the rest of the night had been one to remember.

"I like your friends, the sing-along. I'd forgotten all this existed. Living in Los Angeles is all rush, rush, rush, sleep. Rush, rush, wait in traffic. People hardly have time for friendships, much less nights like tonight."

They skated to the side of the rink to sit on a bench before taking off their skates. "Maybe," he suggested, "you need to make time for all that. For you and for Quinn."

"You're right. I do. But when you're 'in' that world, it's hard to see any other way. I guess that's why vacations are good, right? Life affirming."

"My resort is at your disposal," he said with a gallant bow.

She chuckled. "Why, thank you, kind sir. I will keep that

in mind."

"I really hope you will." Gazing at her under the pale electric lights strung around the rink, he swallowed thickly and kissed her again.

Her lips on his were cool and sweet, and her skin smelled of wood smoke and fresh air and some essence that belonged only to her. Her breasts pressed against his chest as he pulled her closer, made him want her. Need her like he hadn't any needed other woman for the longest time. As if all the years between them, all the mistakes they'd made, were fading behind them.

She seemed to want the same, threading her fingers into his hair, against his scalp—pulling him closer still. But after a moment, she broke the kiss abruptly, breathing hard and pressing her face against the collar of his shirt.

He pulled back. "What?"

"Nothing."

"Tell me. The kiss? I've been wanting to do that all night. Tell me you haven't too."

Tipping her face away from him, she said, "I'd be lying if I said I haven't. But this thing, between us . . . it's . . . it's very complicated. For starters, I live far away in Los Angeles—"

"Are you happy there?"

She shook her head. "That's not a fair question, and it's beside the point. I have a job there, a life. Quinn's in school and—"

"Look," he said, taking her hand. "I know this is something neither one of us expected—this . . . whatever is happening here. But you and I, we've got to be greater than the sum of our past. We've both gone through a lot since then. And second chances don't come around every day. If at all. It's funny that somehow I always knew I'd see you again. Maybe not here, or like this, but something told me we weren't done."

"So," she said, "this is some kind of . . . what? Resolution for us?"

"To the past, maybe. Or maybe a new beginning?"

She sighed. "You're right. I didn't expect this. And there's so much you don't know about me."

Brushing his thumb against the back of her hand, he threaded his fingers with hers. "I know we've both lost people. I know for sure that life is short and that the possibilities that come into our lives are short-lived options. Take this door, not that one. Turn right, not left. Wait five minutes or go now. So maybe we don't say no to whatever this is. Maybe we just say yes to the possibility."

She laid her palm on the side of his face and brushed his beard with her thumb. Then she pressed her lips against his in a gentle goodnight kiss. "You're right. Of course, you're right. But let's talk about this tomorrow. I should go. I need to get back and relieve the babysitter." She leaned over and pulled off her skates.

He nodded. "I'll drive you home."

"I can take an Uber," she argued. "You still have some guests. I'll see you tomorrow."

"They'll understand."

"No," she insisted, slipping her not-ready-for-snow high heels back on. "I'm going to make my own way back. I'm a big girl. I can do it." She glanced up at the dark night sky. "Oh! Look, Cole! It's snowing!"

Sure enough, the white stuff had begun drifting down from the black velvet dome above in big, fat flakes, flickering past the electric lights and melting on their upturned faces.

She held her palm out to catch some. "Do you think it's a sign?"

"Maybe," he said, getting to his feet and pulling her up beside him. "Maybe it is."

NOT LONG AFTER, Eden returned to the hotel and slid her room key across the magnetic swipe at her door. The babysitter, Karen, a forty-something sweet-faced woman, was curled in the club chair reading with a book light when she came in.

Karen held a finger to her lips and pointed to Eden's sleeping son. Eden nodded, then noticed that the book light wasn't the only light in the room. On the dresser, on the spot reserved for luggage or whatever one might bring on vacation, was a small Christmas tree. Fully decorated with twinkling lights and delicate little ornaments of silver and glass.

Karen joined her at the tree and whispered. "Pretty huh?"

"Where in the world—?"

"It was delivered to your room after you left along with a little box of ornaments. Quinn and I had a wonderful time decorating it. Isn't it pretty?"

The ornaments were nearly all animals. Sheep and ducks, dogs and cats. Even a llama or two graced the branches. From one branch hung a little dog that wore a collar with bells that jingled. But it was the playing card that gave away its donor. A queen of hearts. Eden shook her head with a secret smile.

Karen handed her the card that came with the delivery. It read:

Eden and Q,

You can't have Christmas without a tree. Or a dog.

Or at the very least, a little magic.

XO Cole

A rush of *oh, no*! hit her. After tonight, after that kiss and now this. What chance did a girl have? She was in love with him. Really, truly in love with him. And if she was being totally honest, she'd never stopped being in love with him. Despite her mistakes. Despite the choices she'd made for all the wrong reasons. Through all the years they'd been apart, she'd been missing him. And this was why. This little note was Cole. It was everything.

Chapter Ten

COLE HAD SPENT most of yesterday and half of the morning searching for a replacement for Jason Tunney. But with the holiday two days away and such short notice, it wasn't going to happen. Not with anyone big enough to replace his headliner. He'd managed to book some "B" talent, but he knew the audience wouldn't forgive him for advertising what he couldn't provide. Reluctantly, he'd been forced to admit to Granger that things had gone sideways with the concert. Deep down, he hoped his partner might have an idea to save it.

"I hate to say this," Granger told him, standing in front of the window in his office, "but I think our only solution is to consider the offers that have already come in the door. We have four viable buyers."

"No," Cole insisted. "I'm not ready. It can't hurt us to wait until after the concert. Until after Christmas. It will either be win or lose. And by then, we'll know."

"There is not enough snow, Cole," Granger pointed out, gesturing up at the snowmakers on the hill, filling their trails with usable snow. "Despite the flurry last night. What are we supposed to do? *Wish* people up here to ski? We're at a tipping point, business-wise. I don't want this any more than you do. But if we dig ourselves any deeper, we will have no bargaining power when the time comes to actually sell."

Granger's secretary, Sally Haynes, knocked softly on the closed door and popped her head into the office. "Sorry to interrupt. There's a Wesley Russell here to see you? He says he's from Wildwood Acquisitions. Said you'd know what this was about?"

Granger and Cole exchanged confused looks.

"Did you call him?" Cole tried to keep the accusation from his voice, but he was barely holding himself in check as it was. Wildwood Acquisitions was, indeed, one of the companies who'd put in an offer to buy them. They had a reputation for hardball negotiations, if not, possibly under-handed tactics.

"Of course not," the older man answered. "We agreed to wait. I wouldn't go behind your back like that."

Cole nodded at Sally. "We'll see what this is about. Show him in, Sally."

Wesley Russell, a tall, sandy blond millennial who carried the whiff of Ivy League arrogance, walked in with the confidence of a man who already knew he'd won. No doubt his default negotiating position. Two could play that game.

"Wesley Russell. Wildwood Acquisitions," he said by way of introducing himself. "Nice to meet you both in person. Though it's a shame to meet under these circumstances. I know it can be difficult to find yourself in this position." He took the seat they offered but stood slowly back up when neither of them chose to sit as well, but instead, stood shoulder-to-shoulder facing him. He chuckled knowingly. "I see what you did there."

"What exactly can we do for you, Mr. Russell?" Granger asked, moving to pour himself a drink from the small bar beside his desk. "Can I get you something? Bourbon? Whiskey?"

"I never drink this early in the day but thank you. Of course, I'm here about our offer. You have, by now, had a chance to look it over, I assume."

"You made a long trip here all the way from Los Angeles, Mr. Russell. What gives you the idea that we're ready or even willing to field offers from anyone, including you?"

Russell pushed his sports coat aside and shoved his hands into his fine wool trousers. "If you know our company, then you also know how thorough we are. Which is how I happen to know about your concert tonight. The one that Jason Tunney is supposed to headline. When do you plan on telling all your paying customers that he's not coming?"

His question hit Cole like a fist to the gut. No one knew about Tunney except a few staff members and Granger. And none of them would have leaked this news outside these four walls. He had every faith that was true. He remembered that he'd also told Eden. But that was a dead end, he was sure.

"I doubt those guests you're attempting to lure back will

be likely to forgive you for tricking them out of their hard-earned cash. Of course, you could refund them, but that would certainly be a hardship, considering."

"I think we're finished here, Mr. Russell. I'm sorry you went to all this trouble coming all the way up here just to turn back around empty handed—" Cole said, catching the look of angry panic in Granger's eye "—but if you'd called first, you might have saved yourself the trip."

Russell wasn't the sort to be intimidated by anyone. He pulled a sheaf of papers from his inside pocket and laid them on Granger's desk. "Here's our best and final. I think you'll find that it's a little lower than my previous offer. You have until 9:00 a.m. to accept this offer. After that, it's dead. Good luck with the other companies who came forward before. I think you'll find that none of them is still interested in acquiring this particular property now. You see? It wasn't a wasted trip after all. But it will be a quick one. You know this is the best outcome to a bad situation. You know what you have to do. So, do it."

As the door closed behind him, Cole turned to Granger. "He's bluffing."

"What if he's not? And how did he know about Jason backing out? Is word already out there?"

"I don't have any idea how he knew. I haven't even seen any reports on the media about his illness or even about canceling the show. The whole thing smells of insider information. On this end only a few people even know. And none of them would leak that to him."

"Unless Jason himself, or his manager leaked. I wouldn't put it past Ainsley. But Jason?" Granger looked wounded at the very prospect.

"I don't believe that about Jason. I'll get to the bottom of it," he promised. "And when I find out who leaked this—"

"It'll be too late."

Cole plunged his fingers through his hair. "We'll see. Right now, we've got a show to do, and it's too late to fix what's happened. We'll just have to make the best of it."

"And what about his offer?"

"You know what I think about that? And his claim about the other offers disappearing? I think that's stone-cold lie. Let's get past tonight. Tomorrow will come no matter what. Just make sure you're there. I've got a seat saved for you. We're gonna hold our heads up tonight and give them what they came for."

Granger nodded with a bittersweet smile and offered Cole a handshake. "It's been a good run, son. We gave it our best."

Cole pointed at him. "Don't give up on us yet, old man. Not yet."

EDEN AND QUINN were in their room, getting ready to ski, as she had promised him she'd try the bunny slope with him.

It had been years since she'd put on a pair of skis, and she wasn't sure at all she would remember how.

She'd given up on finding Cole before the concert. He'd called, completely buried getting the show ready for tonight. But they'd made plans to meet up before the show because he'd saved her and Quinn special seats. A rush of excitement ruffled through her for what she hoped would be a great night for the resort and for Cole and his partner. There would be time enough after the show to come clean about everything to him, she'd decided. And maybe, by then, he'd have reason to forgive her for not telling him the truth.

Tonight, marked a new beginning for her too. She'd made some decisions that would change her life and her son's. It was amazing to her that a few days away from everything she knew could so remarkably change everything, alter her perspective and give her new courage. Sometimes it took getting away from one's life to really be able to see it clearly. And what she'd seen was how out of balance her life and Quinn's had become and how close she'd come to tipping over an edge she never wanted to with him. Not once since they'd come had he buried his nose in a screen or pretended he didn't hear her when she spoke to him. They'd rediscovered the fun in their relationship, and for that she was grateful.

Not once had she felt that heavy weight that bore down on her daily at Wildwood Acquisitions. Not only because of her self-created mess with Wesley, but with the job itself. If

Nicole could reinvent herself, why couldn't she? It wasn't the end of the world to adjust her trajectory. It was, instead, the beginning of something good.

Standing near the tree Cole had given them, she touched the little glass dog ornament with the bell collar. It jingled beneath the little white lights. The dog reminded her of Mack. Of course, Cole had included a mini-Mack for her son. Even as she warmed to the idea of a dog, she wasn't sure how she could make having one work. And who knew? She'd lain awake last night imagining a future with Cole. Did he want that? Did she?

She reached for the little silver top hat he'd given her the other day and turned it over in her hand.

Watch for the signs, Marguerite had said. *They're left like markers to guide you along the way. If you pay attention. Because the people you love never truly leave you.*

Some people believed that sightings of hummingbirds or butterflies were signs from their lost loved ones. But a Monopoly piece? She laughed to herself. That could only be Jo—if one believed in such things—trying to tell her something. But what?

Running her fingers along the time-smoothed edges, she thought of her friend and said a little silent hello, hoping she could hear. *I've got your son, Jo, and I love him more than words can say.*

Settling the little hat in a prominent branch of the tree, she stepped back and smiled, knowing Jo would approve.

"I can't find my mittens," Cole said, tearing at the clothes in the suitcase.

"They're right here," she said, lifting them off the dresser and handing them to him. "I think we might have to pin those things to your sleeves, so you don't lose them."

"Mom." Quinn looked aghast. "That's for babies."

"You're right. I trust you not to lose them. You ready to go?"

He nodded and pulled open their door.

Standing outside, with his fist raised to knock, stood Wesley Russell.

"Wesley!" A little thread of panic traveled up her body. "What—what are you doing here?"

He propped open her door with his hand and stood in the threshold as Quinn backed up toward her. "Hey, Quinn. You havin' fun with your mom up here?"

The boy nodded but exchanged an uncertain look with her.

"We were just leaving." She started toward the door, but he blocked her exit.

"We need to talk."

"We already have talked, Wesley. You know how I feel." She put her arm around Quinn and pushed him behind her. An instinctive thing. Though she felt silly after she did it. Until he stepped into the room and let the door shut behind him. He'd never given her any reason to fear him. But the look on his face was not one she'd seen before. A mixture of fear, anger, and determination.

She pushed Quinn away and told him to go watch television for a minute. He refused at first, but she insisted. "We'll go in just a minute, okay?"

With the TV on in the background, she stood near the door with Wesley. "What is it you want, Wesley?"

He flicked his brows up as if there was too much to tell about what he wanted or needed from her. "To change your mind."

She shook her head. "No. I won't. It's over between us."

"You're making a mistake, Eden." He reached out to take her hand, but she yanked it away from him.

"My mistake was dating you in the first place," she told him. "We should have both known better."

"People date at work all the time. There are no rules against it in our company."

"Between a boss and his subordinate? Yes, I think there are rules against that. For good reason. But all of that is beside the point now. Because—" she lowered her voice now "—I don't love you, Wesley. Not the way you want me to. It's not going to work out. I'm sorry."

He took her arm in his hand pressing his fingers into her flesh. "What happened between last week and this week? What changed your mind? I want to know."

She stared down pointedly at his hand until he let her go. "I've remembered who I am," she told him. "I've remembered that I need more than settling for checking boxes I thought needed checking. The truth is, you don't want to be a father. I'm Quinn's mother, and he's my priority. For that reason alone, it could never have worked between us."

An offended look tugged at his face. "Who says I don't want to be—?"

"You do. Every time you're with him. It's okay. Not everyone wants to be a parent. But I do. I want to be a good one. And if I choose someone else to share my life with, I want to be sure that person loves my son like I do. I want to feel proud of what I do and who I'm with, for myself and for him. This—us—won't ever be. I'm sorry, Wesley."

A knock on her door, startled them both. Before he could argue, she pulled the door open, leaving him on the other side, out of sight.

Cole stood in the hallway, with a pair of tickets in his hand and a big smile on his face. "Hi!"

"Hi," she said, holding her breath. Oh, God. She didn't want him to see Wesley. She didn't want Wesley to see Cole. Oh, damn.

"I brought you the tickets in case I don't see you before. It's going to be crazy tonight, but I wanted to make sure you got these."

He handed them to her, and she took them, trying to say with her eyes the thousand things should have said but hadn't—and now it was too late.

"Cole!" Quinn leapt from the bed and ran over to the door to hug him. "Did you see the tree you sent us? We decorated it last night, me and the babysitter."

Cole bent to hug him and, of course, Wesley stepped around behind her to face him. As Cole straightened and caught sight of Wesley, his look darted to her in confusion.

"We meet again, Hagan," Wesley said. "And what an interesting place to meet. Right here in my *almost* fiancé's room."

The color left Cole's face as he began to put together pieces that couldn't possibly have made sense before but started to now.

"Cole, I can explain—" she started, reaching out to him, but he pulled away, taking two steps back from her door.

"Yeah?" he said. "How, exactly?"

"It's not—it's not what it seems," she said.

"Yes, it is. It's exactly how it seems," Wesley said. "What? I guess she didn't mention she works for Wildwood Acquisitions. That I sent her here dig up all the dirt on this place that I needed to close the deal?"

His eyes turned on her with accusation, but the horror of Wesley's revelation seemed caught in his throat. And all the while, she shook her head. *No.*

"It was you," he finally managed to say.

"Mom?" Concern and confusion furled her son's brow as he tugged on her arm while trying to interpret this very grown-up disaster unfolding before him. "Cole? What's the matter?"

Cole just shook his head, staring down at the boy.

"I'm . . . sorry, kid."

She shot a pleading look at Wesley to save her, to tell the truth about what had happened, but of course, he wouldn't. She could see he'd managed to put together a story of his own about her and Cole and Quinn. He was just going to let her squirm.

"Cole! Wait—" He'd turned and was stalking down the hallway toward the elevator. "Please! I know how this looks, but just let me explai—"

"You looking for signs, Eden?" he called back at her. "Try that one." And he pointed to the exit sign above the door to the stairwell. That stopped her in her tracks in the middle of the hallway. As if by divine intervention, the elevator arrived on her floor without him even having to push a button and he disappeared into it. The doors slid shut and he was gone.

"I knew there was someone else," Wesley said as he strolled past her in the hallway, hands in his pockets. Turning to walk backward, he sneered at her. "You could have had it all, Eden. But that was your choice," he said, pushing the button on the other elevator. "Oh, by the way, you're fired."

"Oh, by the way," she countered, "I already submitted my resignation to your father this morning. You can't fire me." She turned back to her room, unable to reach her door fast enough. Behind her, she heard the elevator that had taken its sluggish time the entire time she'd been here, ding its arrival with unprecedented promptness. She gave a little prayer of thanks.

Until she reached for the closed handle of her door and found herself locked out. Of course, she was. She jerked the handle and pounded on the door for Quinn to let her in.

As he stepped on the elevator, Wesley smiled and sent her a curt wave. "Goodbye, Eden. Have a good life."

Chapter Eleven

TWENTY MINUTES LATER, as everything was ramping up at the concert venue and Cat and a few others wrangled musicians, Cole found himself walking down the very trail that the sleigh had taken the other night, with Mack off his leash and chasing his favorite yellow tennis ball.

Walking, he supposed, was a generous description of his stride, which left muddy holes behind him. No, he'd covered a lot of ground fast and couldn't get far enough away from the hotel right now to suit him. With the sun sinking into the lee of the mountains fast, he knew it would be dark soon, but he knew these woods well and frankly, he didn't give a damn.

He felt like he'd been punched.

Repeatedly.

In the heart.

Each step took him farther away from understanding what had happened between them. It was impossible to wrap his arms around a betrayal that big. From her. Again. What a fool he was.

Mack ran up to him with the ball in his mouth and

dropped it at his feet. Cole picked it up and heaved it again. Mack did what Mack always did. What a dog was supposed to do. He chased after the ball and brought it back. If only people could be so reliable.

Panting, Mack leaned up against Cole's leg and begged for a pat.

Cole stopped, knelt, and hugged him. Hugged him hard. And the darned dog, he just let him do it. He pressed his face against the dog's fur. "Why, Mack? Why would she do it? What kind of an idiot am I to let her do that to me twice in one lifetime? I wish to God I'd never seen her again."

Mack yawned with a deep whine.

He looked up at the sound of boots crunching snow only to see that woman from the dog park walking toward him with her little emotional support dog, Enoch. She'd managed to appear, as usual, from nowhere.

Cole straightened and stood, turning his face away, as if he was looking for someone or something.

"You lost, *cher*?" she asked as she reached him.

"No." He gathered up Mack's leash to attach it to his collar.

"You look lost," she told him. "Here, you walk with me. I'll get you back. I know where I'm going."

Hell's bells.

"I'm not lost. This isn't a regular trail for guests," he told her. "And you shouldn't be out here so late. Alone."

"I'm not alone. I've got Enoch. And now, I've got you

and Mack too. C'mon, *cher*. Let's turn around and go back where we're supposed to be."

They walked together for a long while in silence, just the sound of their footsteps and the dogs playing together as they trotted along.

"Don't you just love how dogs live in the moment?" she mused after a while. "No matter what just happened or what might happen in a minute, or an hour, or a day, they're happy just to be."

Oh, no, he thought. She was going to philosophize now. As she prattled on about dogs and how brave they were and God knew what else, he looked away into the gloaming light that gilded the tree branches. In the distance he could see the resort, glimmering against the evening sky, the windows lit brightly with Christmas cheer, the eaves hung with greenery.

He thought of the little tree he'd given her. Now he wished he hadn't.

But no. For Quinn, he was glad he had.

Something painful stabbed at him at the memory of the look on the boy's face in that hallway. Like a mirror of his own face, he supposed. All the doubt and incomprehension.

The woman beside him was still talking.

". . . an' I know you haven't heard a word I've said, because you're as deep as a bayou swamp in your own thoughts right now. That's all right, *cher*. That's human. That's what a human bein' does when things go wrong."

"What do you know about what's gone wrong?" he

asked, rather belligerently, he had to admit. "I don't even know you."

She raised her eyebrows with a small smile. "That's true."

He gave a deep sigh. "I'm sorry," he said, meaning it. "I didn't . . . I've had a bad day. I shouldn't take it out on you."

"That's only human too, you know. Like thinkin' a door that closes is actually a closed door."

"A closed door *is*, in fact, a closed door," he argued, with a snort of self-righteousness.

She shook her head with a knowing smile. "That's only what your eyes see, *cher*. Quite unreliable."

"Yeah? Well my eyes have seen plenty, and I don't need anyone telling me I didn't see what I saw. Or know what I know." *Or . . . something like that.*

"But therein lies the problem, *mais oui*?" she said, her strides keeping up remarkably well with his angry ones.

"What? What's the problem?"

She shrugged a little breathlessly. The French say, "*Vous ne savez que ce que vous savez, pas ce que vous ne savez pas.* Which means you only know what you know. Not what you don't know."

This woman . . . He stopped dead on the trail, and she stopped too, a swirl of tiny feathers spinning in her wake. He frowned at them, saying, "I suspect there is some point you're trying to make here, but if you wouldn't mind getting to it?"

Her easy smile broadened. "I thought you'd never ask."

He folded his arms across his chest.

Boldly, she threaded her hand through his bent elbow and urged him forward. Reluctantly, he followed.

"My point is this," she began. "What looks sometimes like failure is often not failure at all, but only what's urging us on to the *right* thing. A closed door, a disappointment or a wrong turn. Or," she added, off-handedly, "a fallible human who might be trying to do the right thing, the wrong way."

She had a sweet, open face, with eyes as bright as the windows up ahead of them, and she spoke of things she had no way of knowing about him but seemed to anyway.

"Who *are* you?"

She laughed. "*Moi*? That's not important, *cher*. Me? I'm just *un vielle* with too much time on her hands, in need of one happy ending."

"Sorry to disappoint you," he told her. "But no happy endings here tonight."

"You know what you need, Boo? A dose o' faith. People will surprise you. They surprise me all the time. And just when you think you know everything, you find out you know nothing."

Not that she knew anything about his life or what he was going through. But if by people she meant Eden, she couldn't be more right. Eden had both surprised him and sabotaged his life in one fell swoop today.

They'd reached a fork in the trail, one side led to the resort and the other to the parking lot and, further on, the town. She stopped with a knowing smile. "This is us," she said, tugging Enoch back in her direction.

"You're not going back to the resort?"

"I might stop by for the concert later. In fact, I most certainly will. But for now, it's time to part ways. For your company and protection, Cole, *bien merci.*"

And off she and her dog toddled into the bright halos of the parking lot lights.

Bereft, Mack stood watching them go, ears up, tail sagging.

"Hey!" Cole called after her. "How did you know my name?"

"That's the wrong question," she called over her shoulder.

Despite himself, he grinned at her irascible logic. "And what's the right one?"

"Oh," she replied, "it'll come to you." And he heard her laugh as she disappeared around a bend in the trail.

FROM BACKSTAGE, COLE watched as bluegrass musicians, traditional choirs, and some local talent, who had returned to this stage as minor celebrities, combined their own style of music with everyone's favorite Christmas favorites at the concert. In the spirit of the holidays, the audience was singing along to the songs they knew so well. Every one of the musicians he'd recruited to come tonight paused in their sets to acknowledge Granger Stuart's essential role in helping their careers along and to thank him personally. He'd sat Granger under a spotlight near the front and he seemed touched and visibly surprised by all the accolades.

He'd let Cat and a few other ski instructors do the honors of MCing tonight. At the last minute, they'd balked at wearing Santa costumes, so they were, instead, dressed in their finest and looking good. But it would be his job to announce Jason Tunney's absence in a few minutes. He wasn't about to put that on anyone else. Several of the acts had agreed to do second sets together in an impromptu jam session he hoped everyone would enjoy, but he wasn't at all sure there wouldn't be a revolt at the box office after he announced it.

Luke Briar and his band were halfway through their set when Cole finally worked up the steel to look out into the audience from backstage. That's when he saw that the two seats he'd reserved for Eden sat empty. Damn. He'd hoped she'd be here to see the results of all her hard work.

A quick scan of the standing room only section came up empty too. Figures. She'd ducked out. Probably hiding in her room until she could catch Russell's private jet back with him tomorrow. She'd left a couple of messages on his phone, pleading with him to call her, but he hadn't answered or called her back. He had enough on his plate tonight without that. Besides, what could she say? She was sorry? Well, so was he.

He kept thinking about that woman on the trail tonight. The one who knew his name. And everything else about him. What had she said? *People will surprise you. They surprise me all the time. And just when you think you know everything, you find out you know nothing.*

He supposed that's exactly where he found himself now. He knew nothing. Except that Eden had come into his life and out of it with a wrecking ball, but he wasn't going to let her knock him down. He'd gotten up before and he'd do it again. No matter how this night turned out.

He glanced out into the crowd again. At the back, near one of the doors, he spotted that smug Wesley Russell, hands in his pockets, waiting. Cole winced at the cold chill that ran through him and he looked away.

Lucy Yarnell, a pretty, dark-haired country singer nearly on par with Jason Tunney sang a heartfelt rendition of "Oh, Come, All Ye Faithful!" backed up by Tom Linderall on piano, a few other musicians, and a local youth chorale that had the audience absolutely swaying to the music. When she finished, she took the mic in her hand. "C'mon up here, Cole!" Lucy shouted, gesturing him up.

Cole braced himself. This was it. He joined her onstage and faked a smile out at the audience.

"This guy here is how this all happened, y'all," Lucy said. "And he did it because of that guy right over there." She pointed to Grange. "Let's have a big round of applause for both of our hosts tonight for putting on this fabulous show." The audience obliged, some standing and cheering. When they quieted, she went on. "Now, some of the musicians here have said a little about how this gentleman got their careers started and how he supported our music by having us in here when we were just baby birds in the music industry, hungry for a break. And I, will be forever grateful to him for supporting me that way. I'm not even from here, y'all! Thank you, Granger, for everything. For believing in me when no one else did. But I want to say a word about Cole Hagan, as well, because we don't want to leave him out."

Cole eyed her warily and spoke into the mic. "That's okay. You can."

The audience laughed but whooped and applauded anyway.

"No, I can't," she said. "Because we all know that you love this place every bit as much as Granger Stuart does and without you, none of this would have been possible. We are thrilled to be up here for the Christmas holidays at the spectacular Four Winds Resort and we hope all y'all out there will plan on comin' back next year for what we expect will be the best skiing on any mountain up here."

Cole took the mic after the audience quieted down. "Thanks, Lucy. Granger and I appreciate all of you more than we can say."

She nodded, and at that point, she was supposed to give him the stage. But she hovered instead. He glanced down at the two empty seats again and went on.

"I know most of you, maybe all of you came tonight to hear this wonderful concert and all these great musicians play, not the least of which was Jason Tunney. But I'm afraid that I have some—"

The audience erupted into a roar of cheering and applause, drowning him out and making him turn to Lucy with a frown. What the—?

He felt a hand on his shoulder and turned to find Jason Tunney himself standing behind him, holding an acoustic guitar and looking healthy.

He grabbed the mic from Cole's hand with a grin. "What he was about to say folks, was you better sit back and get comfortable, 'cause this is gonna be a late night." The crowd roared again. He shouted over the roar. "'Cause I brought Luna"—he held up his old beat-up six string—"and we're gonna mix up Christmas with a few of my newest songs that nobody has even heard yet. What do you think about that?" The crowd could not have been more thrilled to hear it.

Stunned, Cole could only stare at him and Lucy, who seemed in on the whole thing, since she was grinning ear to ear as she walked him off stage. But not before he saw Wesley Russell disappear out the double doors of the exit, looking furious.

Jason started off with his biggest hit, "Someone to Love" that had the crowd on its feet even with the acoustic version, which, to Cole, sounded so much better than the electric anyway.

"That was cruel," he told Lucy holding back a grin. "You knew?"

"Just at the last minute. We were all keeping our fingers crossed he'd make it in time."

"Make it? Wasn't he in Nashville? How? I thought he was sick."

"I think you better hear that from the horse's mouth. Jason wants to tell you himself what happened. But I will say this much, his manager is so fired."

For the first time in hours, Cole took a deep breath and sat down—rather, he lowered himself down—onto a pile of apple boxes propped backstage. *You only know what you know. Not what you don't know.* He guessed she was right about that, at least. Because he had no idea how this had happened.

Lucy sat down beside him. "Did I forget to mention that we—all of us bands—got together and decided not to take any fee at all for tonight? We're donating our performances tonight to the Four Winds."

"What?" He gaped at her. "You're . . . all of you? You mean free?"

"Everyone. Nobody wants to see this place fall into the wrong hands. And everybody trusts you to keep the place going like Granger did. And we all hope we'll be back here many, many times in the future. Merry Christmas, Cole."

Gratitude choked his throat and he hugged her instead of bawling in front of her. "I can't thank you enough. And I'll thank each and every one of them after the show. That's . . . unbelievable. You might have just saved us, Lucy. Does Granger know?"

"He does." She winked at him. "He just wanted you to sweat it out a little bit. He said you were a little out of sorts today. Everything okay?"

"It's a heck of a lot better now."

The show was a smashing success, and the crowd stayed for a second and third encore by Jason and the rest of the bands playing impromptu versions of "It Came Upon a Midnight Clear" and "White Christmas." And it turned out it was snowing outside. Big, fat flakes piling up as all the singing was going on. After all the worry, all the disrupted plans and fear, everything had come together. At least he had this, Cole thought. At least he still had a home.

At the after party following the show for the musicians and bands, where a good hundred people mingled around tables of food and drink, Jason found Cole handing out Christmas cookies to the kids of the local choir that had sung backup with Lucy.

"Jason," he said, handing over the cookie chore to one of his employees. "I don't know what to say. Thank you so much for showing up tonight. Are you feeling okay? We heard you were very sick."

"Nope. I'm fine," he said, slinging an arm around Cole's

shoulders. "I was never sick."

Then why—? "I don't understand."

"I didn't either. You see, Ainsley told me your show had been canceled and therefore, my performance had been canceled. He told me you sent your thanks and regards. And I thought that was weird, but I never dreamed my manager would lie to me about something as important to me as this was. Turns out, he took a little money—a lot of money—from a guy who wanted this show to fail. Someone who wanted to buy the resort."

"Wesley Russell of Wildwood Acquisitions."

"You know about him?"

"It's a long story." One he had no desire to get into here.

"Well, when your friend, Eden, got hold of me—"

Cole jerked a look up at him. "Wait. Did you say *Eden*?"

"Eden Kendall, yeah. These days, I got all kinds of firewalls up to keep folks from getting hold of me directly that I don't want to find me. But she got to me through my mom. Turns out her mom sold my mom some art years ago and they were volunteer friends in Los Angeles. So anyway, my mom calls me and tells me to contact this Eden Kendall ASAP. That it's urgent."

Cole swore silently, began a halting, retracing of the day in his head. The way all of it unfolded like bad dream. His furious response. *It's not what it looks like,* she'd told him. But he'd been too angry to listen.

"So, long story short," Jason continued, "she begs me to

come perform after all and tells me about this Wesley guy and how he operates—bottom-feeder that he is—and once I heard what happened, she sure didn't need to beg me. Somebody needed to hold me back, so I didn't rip my manager's head off when I fired his ass on the phone while he was vacationing on my dime down in St. Bart's."

"She called Russell a bottom-feeder?"

Jason laughed. "In so many words. Yeah. Seems she got taken in by him, just like I did my manager. To be honest, I have a sick feeling now that I'll uncover more of Ainsley's shenanigans once I get back to Nashville and have time to investigate it. But that's my problem, not yours. Anyway, you should know, Eden worked her butt off to book that private jet at the last minute—on a holiday, at her own expense—to pick me up fly me up here to the local airport in time for the show."

"Wait. When did this all happen?"

"Yesterday. That was when she got hold of my mom after callin' everyone else and running into dead ends, and last night we finally talked on the phone. She said something about it being all her fault that this Russell guy had even heard about the concert, but that she wanted to make it right. Fix it, she said. And good as her word, she had a jet waiting for me by 2:00 p.m. in Nashville and here I am. I'm real sorry for the mix up, Cole. I want you and Granger to know that I would never have canceled on him. Never. It was Ainsley who told me not to call, said Granger didn't want to talk to anyone. I thought I'd give him some time before I called him, but I couldn't be prouder to debut some of my new songs up here for your guests. I hope they enjoyed it. And I guess Lucy told you about waiving our fees. That goes for me too. Hell, playing tonight, just me and my guitar . . . it was like old times."

"Thank you for your generosity," Cole said, shaking his hand. But Jason pulled him into a hug.

"If I were you, I'd keep that Eden girl close. She's a real keeper."

IT WAS NEARLY 2:00 a.m. before he found himself in the hallway, walking toward Eden's room. He knew it was late. He wasn't at all sure what he would say to her. *Thank you?* Was that enough? *I'm sorry?*

That struck him as wrong. Should he be apologizing for being angry at her for lying to him? No. But at least he owed her a thank you for doing what she did. At least, he owed her hearing her out, which he hadn't done before.

As he walked down the hallway, he could make out something on the floor outside her door. Catering, maybe? But the closer he got, he saw it wasn't catering at all, but the small Christmas tree he'd gotten them, naked now and lying on its side by the door.

For a long moment, he just stood there, wondering if he

should knock. Wake her up. Which was when Charlie Venner, one of the guys from catering wandered down the hallway, collecting breakfast orders from the doorknobs and cross-checking his clipboard.

"Hey, boss," Charlie said in a quiet voice, plucking an order from the door across the way. "Great concert tonight."

"Yeah, it was. Thanks."

"Everybody's talking about it. How you pulled it off."

Cole nodded, knowing he hadn't done it alone. He lifted his fist to knock on Eden's door.

"I think they're gone," Charlie said, pointing to Eden's door. He double checked his clipboard.

"Are they?"

"Room's vacant on my list. As of this afternoon. Yup. They're gone."

A sinking feeling hit his belly. "Thanks, Charlie. Have a good night. Morning. Whatever time it is."

"Thanks, boss."

So, she was gone. Back home with Wesley Russell? Somehow, after what Jason had told him, he doubted it. But he wasn't sure what to believe anymore. About anything.

Cole's gaze fell to the little Christmas tree, lying by the door. Stripped of all its ornaments and lights, it looked a little sad there, all naked and alone. He wondered if she'd taken the ornaments he'd given to them, or if she'd thrown them out.

Seeing a flash of silver, he bent down and plucked . . .

the little silver top hat from inside the tight branches. The Monopoly piece he'd found in his pocket. She must have forgotten it. Or, more likely, deliberately left it behind.

He turned the thing over in his hand, wondering anew how it had gotten in his pocket in the first place. Wondering, in fact, about all the strange things that had happened since Eden and Quinn had arrived here. The game piece appearing—so connected to Quinn's birth mom; him, falling for Eden again, even knowing what a bad idea that likely was; feeling oddly connected to Quinn from the first minute they'd met; that odd woman with the feather issue . . .

She had, in fact, shown up at the concert. He'd seen her at the end, standing right where he'd seen Wesley standing earlier. But when he spotted her, she wasn't watching the show, but instead, her bright eyes had been on him. When he saw her, he'd smiled, half-expecting a thumbs up in return, or a wave of recognition that she'd been right about tonight. But, instead, she'd folded her arms under her bosom and cocked her head, as if to say, "Well? What now?" Or maybe more to the point, "Now do you believe me?"

Strange one, that woman. And no, he wasn't sure what he believed anymore.

Worse, before today, he'd begun to imagine bringing Eden into his life. Begun to think she and Quinn could share this life he'd created for himself, specifically to prove her wrong about him. Which now felt a thousand times emptier without her.

He walked back down the hallway and stood before the elevator, waiting. His reflection stared back at him in the polished, stainless steel doors. Alone, like him, shaking his head as if to say, "You're a damned fool, Cole Hagan."

Chapter Twelve

ON CHRISTMAS MORNING a few days later, Eden and Quinn, alongside her parents, Tom and Jilly, rode their bikes down the Venice Beach boardwalk on a sunny, cool, beachy day. Quinn, on his brand new blue Mongoose and wearing his new Star Fighter helmet (from her father, of course) raced ahead of them, dodging roller skaters out early on the sand-strewn boardwalk.

"Wait for us!" she called out to him, but of course he was too excited to slow down. She kept him in her line of vision and tried to keep up as they peddled their way back toward their house.

"He'll be fine," Jilly said, pedaling beside her. Her mother's *laissez-faire* style of parenting was in direct opposition to her own helicopter impulses. But she suspected her mother knew something she was only beginning to understand about letting go.

Christmas had dawned like a true California Christmas—with sixty-five-degree weather and blue skies. Her mom and dad had shown up at the crack of dawn to watch Quinn open gifts, of which there were plenty. Of course,

Quinn had been hoping to find a dog inside one of them.

But Eden had clipped out a little picture of a dog and tucked it in an envelope with the promise that they'd go to a shelter to find the perfect dog this week, after giving notice to her landlord. Quinn was positively giddy and insisted that they find that very dog in the picture, a cute, scruffy little character with a smiling face. But she knew Quinn would get over that as soon as he met all the hopeful dogs at the shelter.

It was time, she decided, to find the perfect home for them that could include a pet for her son, who so desperately wanted one. After this week in the mountains, more than a few things had become clear to her.

And now she had a few prospects for work, including a surprising offer from Jason Tunney himself to come to Nashville as his personal assistant. But Nashville was too far from all that she loved, including Quinn's grandparents. Everything would sort itself out eventually, she supposed.

Everything but her and Cole.

Oh, for the last two days, she'd cried on her mother's shoulder plenty, but Jilly, in true Jilly style, had put an optimistic spin on things.

"Maybe this just means you're ready for love, darling. Love in a real way. You know I never thought Wesley was right for you."

"I know. You were right," Eden had told her, sitting on the slip-covered loveseat in her mother's living room. "I was wrong. See? That wasn't so hard."

Jilly laughed, pouring her a cup of tea from the pot she'd just steeped. "Darlin', being right or wrong isn't the point. What's best for you and Quinn, that's what matters. And if you need somewhere to be until you find a new place, well, you can both move in with us." Her hopeful expression made Eden grin.

"I don't think that will be necessary, mom. But thank you." She took her hand and gave it a squeeze. "You know, I look at you two and I think anyone would be so lucky to have a marriage like yours. Forty years strong."

Jilly sighed. "We've had our struggles, but we've loved each other through them all. We've had a good life despite the hard times. Especially because you came into it. And Quinn." Her mother began tearing up and she dabbed her eyes. "Look at me getting all emotional. I just want you to be happy. You'll find someone who will love you like your father loves me. And you'll discover that the rest of it? Well, that will work itself out. It always does."

"I told him I didn't have regrets, but that was a lie. I should never have left him eight years ago. Back then, I thought I knew who I was. What would make me happy. Beyond love. Maybe something to avoid the money traps you two fell into, so I went the other way. I needed a plan. A solid plan, with bullet points." She shook her head over that idiocy now. "I thought the world was littered with pitfalls and I needed to avoid them at all costs, so I didn't end up repeating your mistakes."

Bless her mother, she didn't look offended. "And Cole was one of those pitfalls?"

She shook her head. "Not him. But the life he wanted . . . a life built on passion, not pragmatism. His dreams and mine were just . . . different. He wanted to ski around the world. I wanted to feel secure. Staying with him was a risk I couldn't take. Now I see that the opposite was true. I risked everything to leave him. And now, here I am. Alone again."

"Passion and pragmatism are not mutually exclusive," her mother told her. "Risk is an essential part of both."

She nodded. "That's the regret part. I've realized that it's every bit as risky to deny your passion—your heart—for security, or for money. Wesley taught me that. And more importantly, Quinn. That little boy . . . he dropped into my life like a bomb and exploded all my bullet points, all the mythology I had about what it meant to love someone, to want the best for them. I think the universe laughs at our plans, whatever they are, then has its way with us. I regret being scared enough of where we were heading that I hurt him. Twice. This time, there won't be any second chance."

And Quinn was still a little mad at her for leaving without letting him say goodbye.

Now as they peddled toward home, Eden watched her parents ride beside one another as they always had, laughing and enjoying themselves. She was extraordinarily fortunate to have them still in her life and had a new appreciation for all of it.

In the distance, she watched Quinn stop his bike and hop off, running to the side of the boardwalk. An LA thread of panic shot through her as he disappeared from her line of sight. She peddled faster, catching up with her parents and passing them. But when she reached Quinn, she exhaled in relief. He was sitting on the side of the bike path holding a dog.

Gathering up his bike, she walked it close to him and sat down beside him. "What have you got here?"

"Santa said my dog would find me. Remember? And see? She's lost mom. Look. She just has this old string around her neck. I knew it. I just knew it."

His faith in that stand-in Santa's prediction caught her with unexpected emotion. This dog was, in fact, a scruffy and sweet looking *she*, with a smile that reminded her of that pup whose photo she'd put in the envelope for Quinn this morning. Smaller and certainly dirtier than she imagined any dog they would rescue would be, but clearly in need of help and a good meal.

"Maybe her owner is somewhere nearby," she suggested. "We can't just take her."

"But she wants to come with me," Quinn argued. "Look at her."

Indeed, she was all in on Quinn's lap and she wagged her tail defiantly, daring anyone to say differently.

A passing local with long hair and ragged clothes paused

to watch them and said, "You can take her. She ain't got no home. Just appeared down here a day or two ago, wanderin'. Think somebody dumped her here on the beach. Couple people been feedin' her but, 'til you, nobody could actually catch her."

"Really?" Quinn said. "She just rolled over on her back for me to pet her."

"Well, that means she picked you, then," the man said with a toothy smile.

Quinn beamed up at his mom. "See?"

Jilly and Tom had parked their bikes and came to sit beside them. "Who's this?" Jilly asked.

"This gentleman thinks someone dumped her here," Eden said, scratching the dog behind her ears. Following the thread of her rope collar, she searched for a name tag or a phone number. But her fingers encountered something else under her scruffy little chin. She pulled it around and gasped.

"What is it?" Tom asked.

Between her fingers, was a silver Monopoly game piece in the shape of a baby shoe. "You're kidding me," she breathed.

"Is that . . . a Monopoly game piece?" Jilly asked.

It was just too weird to be a coincidence. She wasn't sure what it meant, except that she half-believed Jo had something to do with this. "There is a thread here, but I'm not sure what it means."

But as this little stray warmed up to Quinn, licking his fingers and taking them all in like they were his family, she guessed this little pup had finally found his boy. And neither one of them would let the other go.

"I suppose if this is your dog, then we should take her home and give her a proper bath. She might be an entirely different color than mud."

"I can carry her!" Quinn said. The dog had other ideas.

As Eden walked both their bike's home, it was clear that little dog wasn't leaving Quinn's side and she trailed all the way back home at his heels.

They reached the corner where her house sat, across the way, a cute little cottage off Main with a front porch and dormers on the roof. The five of them stood, waiting at the corner to cross, bikes in hand as a pickup truck slowly pulled up the street. It was her neighbor, Bob Newland's pickup. Bob was remodeling his kitchen, even on Christmas. There were a pair of sliding glass doors secured upright on the truck bed. Eden waved and he stopped to wish them all a Merry Christmas. As the father of four small kids, she wasn't sure how he kept it all together.

"That's a fine lookin' dog you've got there, Quinn. Is he new?"

"It's a she and I just found her at the beach. She was lost. But not anymore."

He flicked a confirming look at Eden who just smiled. "What'cha gonna call her?"

"We don't know yet." Quinn considered this as he scratched the dog's dirty head.

"Hmmm, she's a Christmas dog, right?" Bob said. "Maybe she needs a Christmas name. Like Cindy Lou Who, or . . . Frosty or . . . Zuzu?"

The dog barked at the last suggestion.

"Are you Zuzu?" Quinn asked her.

She licked his face.

But before anything more could be decided, Eden heard another dog's deep woofing from across the street. Through the sliding glass doors on the truck, she spotted a golden retriever on the stoop in front of her house who looked astonishingly like Mack.

And standing beside him, holding him back was—"Cole!"

Jilly and Tom spotted him too, and looked as surprised as she felt.

"Now, this is getting interesting," Tom said under his breath to his wife. Jilly patted his hand.

Bob wished them a happy dinner and waved goodbye, pulling his truck up toward his house. She and Cole were still on opposite sides of the street as the glass doors slid past. Had he come all the way down here just to see her? A memory of something Marguerite had said to her about sliding doors flitted through her mind and she smiled, feeling her eyes tear up at the sight of him.

"Cole!" Quinn shouted, running across the street to greet

him. "Cole, look! A dog. She just found me, and now she's gonna be all mine. I think her name is Zuzu." Before he could do much more than smile, Quinn peppered him with more questions. "When did you get here? Are you staying for dinner?"

But even as Cole ruffled Quinn's hair, he didn't take his eyes off Eden. "Why don't you give your mom and me a minute to talk and then we'll see. If she'll talk to me, that is."

"Wh-what are you doing here?" she asked as she crossed the street behind her son, taking his shoulders and steering him toward the safety of the curb. Mack seemed elated to see them all, and Tom took the new dog from Quinn to give her a little space.

"C'mon, Quinn, let's go inside and let them talk," Jilly said, rounding Quinn up and guiding him toward Eden's door.

"But—" Quinn argued.

"Because this dog needs a bath ASAP," Tom said, wrinkling his nose. "Merry Christmas, Cole."

"Merry Christmas, Tom. Jilly. And you too, Q."

The three of them, plus Zuzu, made their way into Eden's house, disappearing inside before Cole motioned her over to stand near the low rock wall that ran along the front of her property. All kinds of chaos was pinging through her brain as she dug her fingers into Mack's fur when he leaned against her leg.

"I'm so surprised to see you," she said, as calmly as she

could manage.

"I was going to call you, but this couldn't really be done in a phone call."

Her heart sank a little. He was probably coming to tell her in person what he couldn't manage to say the other day in the mountains. Or, if she was lucky, a thank you for the whole concert thing, right before he dropped the hammer. Well, she deserved whatever he was about to say. And she would simply take it like a woman.

"We might as well get this over with, then. Go ahead. Say it."

He frowned a little. "Say . . . I'm sorry?" With a nod, he added, "I am."

She blinked and canted a surprised look at him.

"Say I should've given you the chance to explain? I should have."

She opened her mouth, but no sound came out.

"Say . . ." he went on, taking her hand in his, "that if I had, I would've realized you were actually trying to help me."

She could not hold back the tear that rolled down her cheek. But still she could hardly speak. "No," she choked out. "I'm the one who should apologize—"

Cole brushed moisture from her cheek with his thumb and pressed a finger against her lips. "Don't cry, Eden. I'm not here to blame you. We both made mistakes. Human mistakes. Because that's what we humans do. But then . . . sometimes we surprise each other—according to a wise woman I met in the woods."

"I didn't think I'd ever see you again." She couldn't stop looking at him, the way his eyes softened when he looked at her now. "I was going to tell you that morning, tell you everything once I'd fixed it, but then—"

"Jason told me what you did. And how all that went down. What you did saved us, Eden. All of us. I don't know what would've happened if he hadn't made it that night. But the Four Winds, it's turning around. We're gonna make it."

She stared at the broken concrete sidewalk. "I'm glad. I'm happy for you. I saw what all those people meant to you. What they meant to each other. It's a family."

"It is. And I love it there. But after everything that happened, after you and Quinn left, it felt a whole lot emptier. Again. So, I got in my car and drove down here with Mack to find you. To tell you that I was wrong. Wrong to not believe you. But you're not an easy woman to find. I went to Wildwood, and they told me you'd resigned."

"I did. It was time for a change in all areas of my life."

"And Wesley Russell?"

She shook her head. "Him, most of all. He was never the right man for me. There's only ever been one right man." She met his gaze. "It just took me eight long years and falling for a little boy who loves dogs to figure it out."

He was standing close to her now. So close she wanted to reach out and touch him, but she didn't dare.

"I really hope you mean me," he said, brushing hair out

of her eyes.

She wondered if he could hear the pounding of her heart, the way it was drowning out everything else. "Of course, it's you. It's always been you." She laughed a little sob. "Even Jo knew that. She tried to tell me that back then, but I was young and confused and thought I knew what I needed. And wanting you would only get me into trouble, throw me off course. But I find I can't control any of it. Least of all, how I feel about you. You were right all along about following your heart. Your passion."

"And you were right to want security. I don't blame you for what happened eight years ago. Our timing was off, that's all."

"We do seem to have terrible timing," she agreed, still not sure where all of this was leading.

"So, let's start over," he said. "Let's move past that and start where we are. I know one thing for sure after all this. I want you in my life, Eden. You and Quinn. I want to spend my days by your side and my nights wrapped in your arms. I want to cook dinners with you and ski down the mountain with you. Take Quinn to football games with you and teach him magic tricks and watch him grow up. If you want to take it slow, we can take it—"

She pulled his face down to her and kissed him. Kissed him thoroughly and well, with everything in her heart, which felt full to bursting. "Yes," she whispered against his mouth. "*Any* way, if that means we're together." He pulled her against him, and kissed her again, deeply and with all his heart, until she felt part of him, and it was hard to tell where she ended and he began. And she knew that somehow this time would be different. No secrets between them. Just a new beginning.

"Get a room!" came a shout from across the street. Two teenaged boys scurried off with laughter. Embarrassed, she and Cole laughed too.

"We should," he agreed emphatically, his vivid green eyes sparkling with humor. And something else much hotter.

"Oh, we definitely will. But for now, come inside." His hand was warm as she took it in hers. "We're having Christmas dinner. And my parents are watching us through the window."

Caught, the older couple ducked behind the curtains.

"They love you." *Impossible, my parents.* "And so do I."

"Well, my love . . ." Reaching into his pocket he pulled something out and put it in her hand, closing her fingers around it. "You forgot something when you left."

She opened her fingers to find the silver Monopoly hat, the one she'd misplaced in the rush to pack. "Oh! You found it. I didn't mean to leave it behind. Thank you." They walked together up the steps to the front door. "You know," she mused, "it's funny. The dog Quinn found? She had a little vintage boot on a string around her neck. Another little game piece. Do you think that could be just a coincidence?"

"Maybe." Cole put his arm around her, considering the

possibility.

Across the street, the bell on the fruit-on-a-stick cart a woman was pushing jingle-jangled continuously as she walked with her back to them toward Main. "*Melones, piña, fresas*!" she called out.

They turned to look and their gazes fell to the bold letters on the side of her yellow painted cart that read, "Marvin Gardens Produce!"

Eden and he exchanged disbelieving glances.

"Then again . . ." he said, walking her toward the door, "maybe not."

"Magic," she mused with a secret smile. "It's a thing. Maybe I'm starting to believe in it."

"Just in the nick of time. It is Christmas after all," he reminded her. "I did bring my Santa beard along, just in case."

She touched his face and the scruff on his jaw she already loved so much. "A good 'ho-ho-ho' will suffice." She kissed him again, right on the front steps of her porch, wishing with all her heart that somehow Jo could see how this all worked out between them.

He smiled against her lips when she came up for air. "Ho-ho-ho. Here's to the beginning of us, Eden Kendall."

"Amen to that, Mr. Hagan," she replied.

And hand in hand, they walked inside to join her messy, would-never-be-ordinary, complicated-in-the-very-best-way family to begin their future over again. As it was always meant to be.

BEHIND THE PRODUCE cart, now nearly to the corner, Marguerite glanced over her shoulder with a knowing smile at the family inside the house. She shook herself, without a single feather coming loose, and whistled for Enoch, who came bounding up from the beach to jump against her legs. "Time to go," she told him.

But with a suddenness that might give any self-respecting angel a start, her young companion appeared beside her, too excited to stay up where she'd left her, and threw her arms around Marguerite.

"*I* thank you," she whispered in Marguerite's ear. "And Aaron thanks you. For everything. You're the best. Here." She pulled a handful of somethings from her pocket and handed them to her. It was the Park Place card and a dozen tiny red hotels. "Though this can hardly repay the debt we owe you."

"Oh, no, darlin'," she told her, pressing them back in her hand. "I already got my reward." She gave herself another shake with a cat-in-the-cream sort of smile. "See?" Not a single loose feather in sight.

"I knew you could do it." She hugged her again and cast a wistful smile back at the house where her boy now lived. "He's alright now, isn't he? They're all alright."

"I do believe they are, *cher*," she said, threading her arm through hers, they started down toward the beach.

"That will make Aaron so happy. I've decided to make this one my new favorite day. Merry Christmas, Marguerite."

The older woman smiled a smile that could only come from the place where kindness grew. "Merry Christmas, Jo."

The End

If you enjoyed this book, please leave a review at your favorite online retailer! Even if it's just a sentence or two it makes all the difference.

Thanks for reading *Every Time a Bell Rings* by Barbara Ankrum!

Discover your next romance at TulePublishing.com.

More books by Barbara Ankrum

The Canadays of Montana series

The Canaday clan is like so many modern families today: blended, flawed and full of love for each other. The series follows the Canaday sisters—Olivia, Kate and Eve—strong yet vulnerable women who have careers and challenges that most of us face as they search for balance in their lives. As is also so often true, their strengths are also their weaknesses when it comes to finding and recognizing true love when it knocks on their door.

Book 1: *A Cowboy to Remember*

Book 2: *Choose Me, Cowboy*

Book 3: *The Christmas Wish*

Book 4: *A Cowboy to Keep*

Band of Brothers series

For the five ex-warrior Navy SEALS who call themselves the Band of Brothers, honor and loyalty are a way of life. But so is the damage each of them faces in the aftermath of the war. They've conquered the physical challenges of the battlefield, but now their struggle is to heal their souls and begin again. Despite the unwavering support of their brothers, each must navigate his own way toward that new beginning. And finding love might just be the key to everything.

Book 1: *Unsung Hero*

Book 2: *Once a Hero*

Book 3: *Unexpected Hero*

If you enjoyed *Every Time a Bell Rings*, you'll love these other Tule Christmas books!

Christmas at the Edge of the World
by Kate Hewitt

Long Lost Christmas
by Joan Kilby

The Christmas Scoop
by Mimi Wells

About the Author

Barbara Ankrum has a thing for the West and has written both historical and contemporary romances, all set in that magical place. Twice nominated for RWA's RITA Award, her bestselling books are emotional, sexy rides with a touch of humor. Barbara's married and raised two children in Southern California, which, in her mind, makes her a native Westerner.

Thank you for reading

Every Time a Bell Rings

If you enjoyed this book, you can find more from all our great authors at TulePublishing.com, or from your favorite online retailer.